Dangerous Testimony

Dana Mentink

HARLEQUIN® LOVE INSPIRED® SUSPENSE

Recycling programs for this product may not exist in your area.

ISBN-13: 978-0-373-45699-4

Dangerous Testimony

This edition published by arrangement with Love Inspired Books.

www.Harlequin.com

Printed in U.S.A.

For God hath not given us the spirit of fear;
but of power, and of love, and of a sound mind.

—*2 Timothy* 1:7

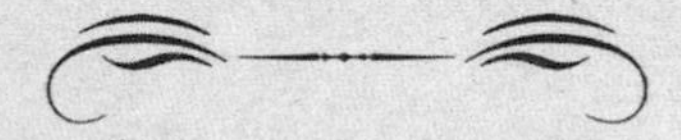

For those who bravely tend to home and family while their loved ones serve in our military. God bless you all.

ONE

A loud pop.

The flash of the gun.

A man's body crumpling to the unforgiving cement. Not a man, a boy, barely old enough to shave, by the looks of him. A boy, somebody's son, gone in the split second it took to pull the trigger. He'd had brown eyes and full cheeks, maybe the kind that dimpled when he smiled, like her daughter Tracy's. But he would never smile again.

Candace Gallagher Andrews blinked the memory away for the thousandth time. "It's over," she told herself fiercely. "He's dead and they arrested the shooter four months ago, so let it go and do your job, you ninny."

The incident had left her with a lingering echo of fear, a feeling she detested. After a few slow breaths, she stowed her iPad in her bag, locked the car and straightened her suit jacket. She'd found a parking place three blocks from the college. Though it was broad daylight in a very public place, she hurried anyway, eager to be enveloped by the safety of others. "Maybe you should have let Marco come," she muttered under her breath. He had all but insisted in that pushy way of his.

Typical Marco. The former navy SEAL and longtime family friend sorted everything and everyone into precisely two camps: friendlies and enemies. She'd made enemies when she agreed to testify against Kevin Tooley, a member of the Wolf Pack, the murderer who'd gunned his rival down right in front of her. But she'd had no choice. If she let the shooter go unpunished, what kind of person was she? What kind of mother? Backing down would not show the honor and courage her husband, Rick, would have modeled for their daughter before his death.

"It's a presentation at a community college," she'd proclaimed with some bravado. "I'll be perfectly safe, and besides, you scare people."

Marco continued to be a rock in so many ways as things had gone from bad to worse for the Gallaghers. Their father's death was just the beginning of the family trials as the Gallagher sisters encountered one frightening scenario after another, until the most recent, when Candace had witnessed the shooting outside a gas station. At least her seven-year-old daughter had not been with her. God had spared them that. Tracy's life had been impacted enough by violence already. Half a world away, in Afghanistan, it had robbed Tracy of her father, and Candace of the only man she'd ever loved—goofy, patient, faithful Rick.

Candace walked the last two blocks, the Southern California sun flushing her cheeks, even in the month of October. Dumb idea to wear a suit jacket in Long Beach, but the tan color complemented her brown eyes and made her feel professional, in the same way mashing her curly hair into a chic twist had done. Teaching a session on investigation techniques to eager criminal justice majors was just the thing to promote the company and keep her mind off the upcoming trial preparations.

It was late morning, and she was surprised to see very few people ambling along. A car crept slowly by, and she froze for moment, clutching her bag, recoiling in spite of herself. Would the tinted glass roll down in a thunderous explosion of bullets? Her heart hammered against her ribs as the window slowly lowered.

"Do you know where the post office is?" the elderly driver asked.

Candace pushed the words through her dry mouth. "Another block down, make a left. You can't miss it."

The car drove away, and Candace stood there, breathing hard, feeling ridiculous beyond words. Was this fear ever going to go away? Probably not until the trial was over. She'd just have to do her best to keep it in check. Her sister Angela, who was dealing with PTSD from her service as a navy chaplain in Afghanistan, told her it would take time to heal.

Time Candace would rather spend taking care of Tracy and working as a private investigator.

Nearing the school boosted her confidence. She straightened her shoulders and held her head high. As she crossed the narrow alley, tires squealed and her attention was drawn to a car slamming to a halt, someone flinging the passenger door open. This time it was not her imagination. She vaguely recognized the face, the driver of the car who had stopped just long enough at the gas station to allow his passenger to kill a young boy. He had managed to elude the police.

It was him, all right, and his intent was clear.

Run, her mind screamed. *Run or die.*

Marco ground his teeth in frustration. Traffic resulted in such a delay that he'd not been able to insert himself into Candace's outing to Long Beach.

He shot a glance at the big dog sprawled in the passenger seat, happily oblivious to traffic or anything else. Bear was happily oblivious to most everything, unless he was taking direction from Marco. Then it was another matter entirely for the black-and-tan Malinois. Marco had worked with a fellow SEAL one time who was just like that. Most relaxed guy you'd ever see…unless he was on a mission. Then he was a force to be reckoned with…and surrendered to.

Marco was hungry, and annoyed that Candace had not listened to him. What was it about women that made them constantly disregard his advice? He'd served in eight SEAL Platoons, was platoon chief in five, and awarded the Navy and Marine Corps Medal for Heroism, but could he get any woman anywhere to listen?

And the Gallagher sisters, Sarah, Angela, Donna and now Candace, were trouble magnets. After Sarah's recent kidnapping and Angela's life-and-death struggle in Cobalt Cove, he felt like snapping GPS trackers around the Gallagher sisters' wrists whether they liked it or not. At least Donna had the Coastie keeping an eye on her when he wasn't on duty, and Sarah had Dominic Jett, a kid with guts enough to be an explosive ordinance technician before he'd gotten injured. And Angela was planning to marry the doctor. Marco huffed. Dr. Dan was okay for a civilian, he had to admit, but still. Wasn't like the guy had ever handled a grenade launcher or an assault rifle or anything.

Part of him had to smile at the way the Gallaghers bested him on a regular basis. Though he'd never admit it to any of them, he admired their spirit, even though they drove him to distraction.

Creeping along, he finally found street parking opposite the campus and dialed Candace's cell phone. She didn't answer.

He sent her a text, big fingers fumbling over the tiny buttons. Here.

No reply, so he reached for the door, hand freezing in place as he caught sight of Candace fleeing down the alley and a dude in baggy pants with a backward baseball cap running after her.

"Bear," he said, as he leaped from the driver's seat.

The dog sat up, ears swiveling.

"Time to go to work."

* * *

Candace sprinted down the alley, which led to a small parking lot behind the school. There had to be a back door where she could get into the building, or a late arriving student whose attention she could attract. Breath coming in pants, she dodged behind a parked compact car and tried to calm her thudding heart so she could listen.

She tried desperately to focus. Had she heard the sound of running feet? She slid a hand in her bag to rummage for her phone, but the cell had slipped to the bottom and she couldn't lay her fingers on it. Oh, why hadn't she cleaned out her bag like she'd been meaning to? Should she run to the building or wait for help? Neither option was attractive.

Come on, come on, she pleaded silently. *Somebody come along. It's a public building. Where's the public?* The squeak of sneakers made her skin erupt in goose bumps. Peering under the car, she couldn't see the location of her pursuer.

A smattering of litter had collected along the periphery of the lot, and a brown rat was padding its way through the mess. In the far corner of the parking lot she heard the familiar beep of a car lock being activated.

Hope rising, she peeked up over the hood to see a tall, lanky young man in a sweat jacket striding toward the building. She ached to call to him, but again the fear left her mute. *Stay hidden or get help? Which one, Detective Candace?* Seconds ticked by until she let her instincts take over. Darting from behind the car, she ran toward him. "Help," she yelled. "Help me."

He did not turn.

"Help!" she cried, throwing aside all attempt at caution, waving her arms and hollering. "Please."

She realized too late that he had earbuds firmly in place and couldn't hear her. Her only chance to get to the back door and help was to run toward him and hope her pursuer wouldn't want to risk dragging others into the situation.

She took off in a sprint. Fueled by terror, she ran faster than she thought she could. Each foot she gained ratcheted her hope a little higher, until the man suddenly detached himself from the shadows, hooked a leg around her ankle and sent her sliding to the asphalt. Her palms hit the ground, the rough surface grinding into them as well as her bare knees. Through the pain, she kicked out, making contact with a shoulder or face—she couldn't be sure which.

He grabbed her from behind, fingers wound in her disheveled hair, bringing her to her feet and slamming her over the hood of the car.

"You scream, you die," the man hissed in her ear, his breath sour on her cheek.

He pulled something from his pocket and held it in front of her eyes. With a snick of sound, the switchblade opened. The razor-sharp edge gleamed, and fear cut into her as deeply as the blade soon would.

Stubborn determination bucked like a mule past her panic as she thought of Tracy, her little girl who'd already lost her father. There was no way Candace was going to lie here and get her throat cut without the biggest fight of her life. Rick would have said to resist with her last ounce of strength. She intended to.

Lord, help me, she prayed. *Let me go home to my daughter.*

Her assailant leaned back slightly. The movement opened a tiny window of opportunity. Before the fear took over completely and paralyzed her, she made one last desperate attempt to save her life.

Marco jogged down the alley, Bear trotting next to him. They stuck to the shadows, taking it all in. A kid at the far end of the lot had just entered the building, oblivious, sipping coffee from a plastic cup, earbuds no doubt crammed in his ears.

Where are you, Candace?

He didn't hear the sound, but Bear did. The dog went rigid, tail erect, nose quivering.

Marco gave him the command to "go quiet" and the dog dashed through two rows of parked cars. Marco caught up in time to see Candace rear up off the hood of a parked compact, smashing the back of her head into the face of an attacker. The goon reeled back, hand reflexively going to his bloody nose. It gave her the time she needed to sprint away. The guy spun to catch her again, and Marco saw a switchblade in his hand.

"Here!" he called to Candace as he ran toward her. Wide-eyed with terror, she raced to him. He shoved her behind, his body shielding hers.

Bear was barking wildly now, as the bloody-nosed kid turned to Marco, but the dog had not attacked yet because Marco hadn't told him to. Not bad for a new trainee. Marco regarded the guy calmly. "Put it down."

"Uh-uh," the kid said, hands out, the blade ready in one of them, his gaze darting between Marco and the dog.

Bear barked and lunged forward a step.

"I'll cut your dog if he comes near me, 'fore I cut you."

Marco picked up a slender board that was lying against the brick wall. "That would not be wise." He smiled. "I don't want my dog to get dirty biting you. I just bathed him."

"This isn't your business," the kid hissed, jerking his head at Candace. "She's messing with the Pack, and Rico wants her to stop."

"Ah. So your boss sent you. I didn't figure you were a decision maker." Rico was the Pack leader, dangerous, unpredictable and wily. He'd apparently decided to scare Candace off testifying against Kevin Tooley. Marco kept his voice light. "Tell your boss that his boy Kevin is going to prison for that gas station shooting, so he'd better learn to accept it."

The kid looked nervous now, his knife hand dropping a few inches. Marco waited until Bear barked again, momentarily drawing the kid's attention. Then he swung the board as if he was Babe Ruth driving one out of the park.

The board impacted the guy's wrist with a thwack, sending the switchblade pinwheeling through the air, as the thug grabbed his arm and howled in pain. The back door of the school slammed open and a security guard hastened out, shouting into his radio.

Still holding his wrist, Candace's attacker shot Marco a look that promised revenge, and then took off toward the rear of the parking lot.

"Bear, chase," Marco said.

The dog tore after the youth, who ran as fast as his baggy pants would allow.

He hurled himself up over the fence, Bear biting madly at his shoe. One sneaker came off, and Bear snatched it up, still barking in a volume that echoed through the whole space.

"Cops are on their way," the security guard called out. "Need an ambulance?"

Marco turned to Candace. Her face was stricken, body trembling and a bruise developing on her cheekbone, which made him want to take another swing at Shoe Guy.

Her brown eyes were terrified, a sight that cut deep down to his core. *I told you I should have come along*, he wanted to say. *Why don't you ever listen to me?* Instead, he bent and gathered her in his arms, taking her fear and willing it away, thanking God she was alive.

"Gonna be all right," he murmured, holding her tight.

"Jay Rico wants me dead." Panic shot through her

words. "Marco, what about Tracy? What if he sends people after us both?"

He squeezed her closer, every protective nerve in his body firing on all cylinders. It was a struggle to keep his voice level, calm, when there was a flood of anger roaring through him like a storm-tossed surf.

"No one is going to hurt you or Tracy," he said through gritted teeth. "No one."

TWO

Candace sighed. Resistance was futile. Marco was not about to let her drive back to Coronado by herself.

"We'll get your car home another way," he'd proclaimed.

The best she could do was climb into the passenger seat of his truck and cram next to Bear. The dog was chewing a white shoelace as if it was a savory strand of fettuccini.

"Don't the police want it for evidence?"

Marco shrugged. "They agreed the shoe was enough. No one wanted to persuade him to relinquish the lace."

"You could command him to."

"Yeah, but he did good work today and I pay him in kibble, so he deserves a prize. They've got the switchblade and the shoe, anyway."

She gazed out the window as they drove over the Coronado Bridge, back to the gorgeous island that seemed extra welcoming now. The fall sunlight bathed the palm trees in rich hues and she rolled down the window to let in the cool ocean air. It all seemed so much more vibrant, so precious.

Nearly having your throat cut made you appreciate things more, she thought ruefully. *Thank You, God, that I'm still here to savor this.*

When they drove past the street that led to her bungalow, she shot Marco a look. "Why aren't you taking me home?"

He had the decency to appear slightly chagrined. "Your mom's orders. She doesn't want you staying alone tonight. Tracy's already camped out in her guest room. She's right, you know."

"I want to go home," Candace said, trying not to sound like a petulant child. "To my house. I'm thirty-three years old and I don't have to do what my mother says anymore."

He raised an eyebrow. "Well, I'm thirty-six and I do, so here you are."

She huffed out a breath. "Did you always do what your mother wanted?"

"Of course." He was the picture of innocence.

"Uh-huh. I'm sure all moms want their sons to become navy SEALs. She probably wished you'd become an orthodontist."

He chuckled. "Can you picture me as an orthodontist?"

Marco's strapping shoulders and massive hands painted him as more of a linebacker type. "Not really. Are you coming in?"

He shook his head. "I've got something to take care of."

His eyes were the color of toffee with shimmers of copper in them. They had always fascinated Candace, because she couldn't understand what went on behind them. She knew he was keeping his plans from her, and further, she knew it would do no good to try and pry them out of him. He would or would not share at the proper time. Now he was also plotting ways to ensure her safety from Jay Rico and his Pack, no doubt.

She reached over Bear and touched Marco's biceps, rock hard under the tight material of his T-shirt. So warm. Even on the coldest days. The electric buzz it awakened in her nerves confused her. She wanted to both prolong the touch and back away at the same time. She laced her fingers in her lap. "Marco, thank you." She sucked in a breath. "You were right."

His mouth quirked. "Hold on. Let me get my phone. Can you say that again so I can record it?"

"I mean it. I should have listened to you. The Pack really is determined to scare me away from testifying against Kevin Tooley next month."

He waited a beat. "Have they succeeded?"

A long moment passed while she considered her scraped knees, the glitter of the switchblade in her attacker's hand, the hot flush of panic, the moment when she'd thought she might not live to see her daughter again. What followed was an explosion of anger in her soul, a solidification of her resolve, like cement hardening. Rick had always said she was a pussycat with tiger stripes.

"No one is going to frighten me into backing down."

Marco smiled, a wide boyish grin that turned the copper in his eyes into molten streaks.

"Spoken like a true Gallagher."

"Who is still bossed around by her mother."

He laughed. "Even a fleet admiral follows his mother's orders. No one outranks her."

Candace squeezed his wrist. "Really though. I probably wouldn't be sitting here if you hadn't been there."

He nodded, staring out the front window, his face quickly shuttered.

"Will you be in the office tomorrow?"

"Meeting in the conference room at 0600 to nail down our strategy. Gonna do a little research tonight."

"Research?" Her heart thudded. "Marco, you're not going to go track down any gang members, are you?"

"Just some initial recon."

She realized suddenly that her decision to testify had put them all in danger. Under her fingertips his pulse was sure and steady. He was not letting fear take hold and neither would she. "Please be careful."

"I am always careful. You, however, are not. Don't go anywhere by yourself. Brent will take you and JeanBeth to the office tomorrow. Bring Tracy."

She gave him a sassy salute. "Yes, sir."

"Sorry. I meant to put a 'please' in there somewhere."

"I know, but that doesn't come easy because you're naturally bossy."

He nodded. "Yeah, so you've told me."

"Still...don't put yourself in danger, okay?"

He answered with a silent nod, waiting until she went inside before he drove away. Watching from the window, she whispered a prayer for Marco and went to find her daughter.

The next morning at 6:00 a.m., Marco carried a sleeping Tracy from Brent's truck and laid her gently on the couch in the reception area, where Candace tucked her in. It got to him, looking at Tracy's delicate freckled profile, watching Candace stroke her fine blond hair. So small and innocent. The idea that someone, anyone, could possibly attempt to rob Tracy of her mother nearly sent him over the edge.

"Morning." Baxter, the sixtysomething custodian with the graying fringe circling his bald pate, tiptoed out with a bag of trash. The bag was so full that Marco stepped up to help him with the load.

"I got it," Baxter whispered, to avoid disturbing Tracy. "Have to earn my keep."

"You do, Baxter, every day," Candace said.

Marco agreed. Though he'd been there only a few months, Baxter was the best custodian the building had ever had. Score one for the mature guy, Marco thought. Plus he had been known to bring in detective books for Tracy that he'd read to his nephew a decade before, and that got him extra points in Marco's estimation.

"Early meeting usually means trouble," Baxter said, raising a grizzled eyebrow.

"Nothing we can't handle," Marco said.

Baxter gave him a cocky salute as he headed for the door. "I believe that."

Marco and Candace crept out of the reception area and joined the others.

Marco looked at the group seated around the Pacific Coast Investigations conference table—dark-haired Brent, with his arm around Donna, Angela without the company of her fiancé, Dr. Dan, and the sisters' mother, JeanBeth. The only sister missing was Sarah, who was currently honeymooning in Hawaii with her new husband, Jett. All of them had resisted filling the newly married couple in on the situation. They were entitled to some uninterrupted joy, having recently survived being abducted and held on an island for nearly a week. Sarah would throw a monster fit at being left out of the loop when she returned, but that wasn't a problem for today.

Marco cleared his throat. "Met with a couple of guys. They told me where I might be able to find Jay Rico. He's the big boss of the Pack. We have to get to him to stop the threats against Candace."

Candace gasped. "Oh, no. That's a bad idea, a very, very bad idea."

"Gonna take me a while to confirm," Marco went on. "In the meantime…"

"We do a complete investigation into anything and everything having to do with Jay Rico and his Pack," Donna finished.

"Right," Marco said. "Their members, their arrest records, their funding sources, everything."

Brent nodded. "I have a buddy in Homeland Security. He owes me a favor."

"Call it in," Marco said.

"Yes, sir." Brent pressed a kiss on Donna's temple before he rose.

"Isn't anyone hearing this?" Candace said. "Marco, you

are not going to search out Jay Rico. Let us investigate and do our jobs. It won't accomplish anything to go after him."

"He's the lead hostile. Need to go serve him notice."

"No, you don't," she said, eyes flashing. "I'm not going to have you getting killed."

The fire in her tone made his heart thud harder. She didn't get it. He would risk anything, take on anyone, to keep her and Tracy from harm. These people—these women around his table and the child sleeping in the next room—gave him a purpose. They were his life and nothing mattered more to him than they did.

"Not going to get killed. Not by a two-bit gangster like Rico."

All of a sudden, her expression changed, and he thought he saw her lips tremble. He wanted to pull her close. The urge was not in keeping with his resolve. *It's a mission, like any other.* But Candace was not a woman like any other. Even though he loved all the Gallagher family, Candace occupied a different part of his soul, though he didn't like to think about it. He drank a gulp of water to cover his confusion and stowed the feelings away in that deep-down place where he put all the other uncomfortable things in his life.

There was a soft knock at the door.

Marco opened it to a skinny man with long dark hair pulled back in a ponytail, an affable smile on his face. He bobbed his chin by way of a greeting.

"This is Lon," Marco said. "He's going to keep watch on JeanBeth's place." Marco quickly introduced the group, ignoring the surprised looks.

JeanBeth, the consummate military wife, rose without batting an eye and offered Lon a seat, which he politely declined, and a glass of water, which he also refused.

Candace was not as serene. She wasn't a fan of surprises, Marco had come to learn, and this one would be hard for her to swallow. "It's nice to meet you, Lon, but Marco, would you mind explaining?"

"Lon and I served together."

Marco felt it was an adequate explanation. Candace did not, from the crimp in her full lips. Her mahogany eyes flashed in that way that made his stomach muscles tighten.

"So now you've gone ahead and arranged for soldiers to guard my mom's house?"

"Lon's on medical leave for a torn ligament. He gets bored. Needs something to do besides play video games."

Lon smiled.

"You've brought in help." Candace's eyes narrowed. "Without bothering to consult us? Is there anything else we should know? Did you enlist any more of your buddies to guard my house, too?"

Marco tidied the already neat stack of papers in front of him. "Possibly."

Candace groaned. "This is ridiculous, way out of proportion. I'm going to be careful and keep a close eye on Tracy. We'll be extra cautious until the trial is over. We don't need a platoon of people."

"A platoon is sixteen. We're closer to a squad," he said, to clarify.

She groaned. "You're not listening to me."

"Yes, I am, but this is serious."

"Overkill."

"Your father would have done the same."

She flinched and he wished he hadn't said it. Bruce Gallagher's death was still a raw and painful wound for all of them. *But I can't let anything happen to you, don't you see?*

She closed her mouth. "Fine. Do whatever you want. You will, anyway. I'm going to check on Tracy."

It bothered him to upset her, and he didn't want to bark orders as if he was her commanding officer, but he couldn't give voice to that softer, disconcerting thought. *Seeing you hurt would be unbearable.*

He couldn't take it, not after Gwen. She'd never in the four years they'd been married come close to staying clean, even after he'd wiped out his savings on rehab programs. Married when they were both just eighteen, she'd endured his navy boot camp days and the moving around, fighting battles he'd not fully comprehended until the addiction took hold. Then they'd fought together, but no amount of muscle, determination or grit could free her from the enemy of heroin. Or maybe he could have fought harder on his home turf instead of giving himself to the navy. He'd served his country, choosing to believe that he'd changed things, helped her, saved her. He'd been dead wrong.

There had been moments of pure joy, when he'd been sure they would make it, and deep down, part of him believed it right up until the moment she'd sent him a letter two months into his deployment, telling him she'd pawned her wedding ring and filed for divorce.

The thing that scared Marco the most was that he would have still tried to save their marriage, because despite the torture, he loved her and he always would. Even after the papers were signed, after her belongings were stripped out of the base housing they shared, even as a twenty-three-year-old divorcee whose ex-wife had cleaned out their bank account—even then, the love inside him was greater than the hurt. The divorce was a defeat, the worst he'd ever experienced, a public exposure of his failure. But still, he'd had the navy to bury himself in, and what had Gwen had? When he'd learned of her recent death from an overdose, he'd been anguished to his core, a feeling that still stabbed him in the gut when he let it.

He blinked, realizing he'd missed the last few comments.

Pay attention, Marco. What's the matter with you?

With the briefing over, JeanBeth returned to the house with Lon, reminding them she would expect the entire group for lunch. They scattered to their respective corners, fingers tapping on keyboards and dialing phones. Determined to keep his mind on the critical business at hand, Marco marched off toward his own cubicle, itching to shut down Jay Rico before he could cause any more grief.

THREE

Candace watched Marco settle himself in the office chair behind his cubby walls and poke the computer to life, staring at the screen. He detested computers, and it was only after painful hours of her tutelage that he had become proficient on the new office email and messaging system. Still, he faced the screen as if it was a wily adversary bent on destroying him. As she considered his strong profile, muscled body dwarfing the small cubicle, she wanted to stay angry at him, to resent his cavalier treatment of her life, his tendency to order instead of ask. She wanted to keep her ire burning, but she found as she looked at him that she couldn't.

"Marco," she said, after a deep breath. "I know you want to protect me and Tracy, and I appreciate that, but don't you think you're taking this to an extreme? Recruiting your navy buddies?"

He didn't turn around, quickly replacing a photo he'd been looking at in its usual place. After a moment he said, "No."

She sighed. "But it's crazy."

"Not crazy to protect people you care about."

Something in the words spoke of profound regret, drawing her closer. She saw the little black-and-white photo on his desk that he'd just replaced. The picture showed a proudly smiling young sailor, his arms around a willowy blonde woman who would later ruin her life and his with drugs. Gwen.

"Marco, what happened to Gwen wasn't because you didn't protect her."

He stiffened, eyes still locked on the screen, and she knew she'd struck at a wound by mentioning Gwen's name.

"Yes, it is. I wasn't there enough," he said after a moment.

The way he'd loved the broken Gwen, the way he still loved her memory even after the punishment she'd inflicted, made Candace's heart break just a little. She moved closer and wrapped her arms around his shoulders from behind. She could barely grasp him across the solid torso as she breathed in the scent of soap and pressed her cheek to his neck. "You couldn't have saved her, not from that."

"Yes, I could." It came out as a whisper.

He still believed he'd failed his wife, the shame trapping him in a past from which he could not escape. Wishing she could somehow siphon the pain away, Candace savored the hard planes of his jaw. "You are a good man, Marco Quidel."

She thought she felt him relax a fraction, lean his head ever so slightly into the softness of her embrace. But he did not turn, and he didn't answer, so she pressed a kiss to his hair and left.

Marco allowed himself a couple hours of research and phone calls before he decided to run with Bear in tow to JeanBeth's home, which was only two miles from the office. The others had already departed. He hoped the exercise would clear his head. First off, he couldn't seem to rid his stomach of the tilt Candace's embrace had caused. It was an unwelcome feeling. Candace was like family, a woman to be protected, not...well...attracted to.

Attraction? That was absolutely not what caused the stomach tilt, he told himself. Probably it was due to some residual tension set into motion by the parking lot attack.

He was more comfortable with the subject of attacks than attraction. Whether Candace accepted it or not, she was in danger and so was Tracy. He would convince her of it if it was the last thing he did. His pace accelerated, and Bear kept up easily.

The Coronado sky was a breathtaking blue and San Diego Bay dotted with pleasure craft. A freshening wind against his face made him yearn to take Candace and Tracy out on his boat, the *Semper Fortis*, and listen to their cheerful chatter as they fished for bass in the bay. The boat never seemed to be as filled with life as it was with the two of them aboard, but it would have to wait until they put away Rico and his goons. It angered him that Tracy would miss out on school and her friends because of Rico, maybe even her upcoming birthday party. Somehow Candace would explain it to Tracy so it made sense to an almost-eight-year-old.

How did Candace do it? he wondered. Serve as both mother and father to Tracy. The kid was turning out great as far as he could see. How could she not with a mother who was so filled with grace, and determination and love? Candace was a rock for Tracy, and for some reason, she calmed a restlessness inside him, too, like nothing else did. Again the stomach tilt. He soothed himself by reciting parts of the creed embedded in his soul, even though he no longer wore the SEAL trident.

I will never quit. I thrive on adversity.

Honor on and off the battlefield.

My word is my bond.

His bond. His gut twinged. Long ago he'd promised Gwen he would love and protect her forever. He had not been able to shield her from the wicked hold of addiction. Would he be enough to protect Candace now?

He slowed the last two blocks and Bear reduced his gait to a steady trot. *Watch and observe, Quidel. Stick to the mission, keeping Candace and Tracy safe from the Pack. You're going to win. You have to.*

"You're gonna to listen to me this time, Candace," he said as he eased his pace to a walk, knocked once and tried the door, surprised to find it locked. JeanBeth had an open-door policy, so Lon must have changed her ways. *Atta boy, Lon.* He used his own key to let himself in.

Tracy looked up from the board game she was playing with Lon, and ran to give him the customary squeeze. "Hi, Unco."

Lon lifted an amused eyebrow, which Marco ignored.

She'd called him that since she was two years old and he'd returned to Coronado on leave. Crossing paths with Bruce Gallagher meant an invitation to meet his family, and they had taken him under their wings. Those were happy times back then, before Rick had been killed and Marco had been christened Unco. No one else in the world would dare address him like that. It made him sound like a jolly grocer from a kid's story, but from Tracy, he didn't mind. For some reason he couldn't manage to be very stern with the girl, who made him laugh like no one else on earth.

"Who's winning?" he inquired.

"I am," Tracy announced proudly, "But Mr. Lon is trying his best."

Marco chuckled. "You're going down, Lon. Kid's an ace at checkers."

Tracy beamed. "Only sometimes." She turned to Lon. "Want to take a break and go throw the ball for Bear in the yard?"

"Uh-huh," Lon said, and Bear, sensing a game in the offing, was quick to follow them to the back sliding door and out into the Southern California sunshine.

JeanBeth handed Marco a plate full of kale salad with

cranberries and lemon vinaigrette. His favorite and she knew it. They settled in the living room.

"Lon doesn't talk very much. Is that some sort of Navy SEAL creed?" JeanBeth asked.

Marco smiled. "No, I know a few guys who will talk your ear off if you bring up the right subject."

"What's the right subject with Lon?"

"Dunno. I've never figured that out."

"He doesn't eat much, either," she said with a disapproving frown. "Look how thin that man is. If he turns sideways you can't even see him."

"When we were stationed in Virginia Beach his mom sent him fudge. He's got a real sweet tooth."

Her face brightened. "I'll make a note of that," she said. Marco sensed that JeanBeth had just assigned herself a different kind of mission altogether. *Brace yourself, Lon.*

Brent slung an arm around Donna and leaned back on the couch.

"The Pack doesn't leave much of a trail," Brent said. "My guy at Homeland put me in touch with a Fed who figures Jay Rico runs a series of chop shops, but the locations change and they haven't been able to get a bust."

Candace nodded. "That's what Donna and I got, too. We did find out that Rico was born in Long Beach, and he had a brother who died in jail and a sister who seems to have dropped off the radar. Never married. No kids."

The phone rang, and JeanBeth picked it up and said hello.

Marco eyed her, noting the tension in her jaw as she listened, the subtle stiffening in her posture. She put the phone down.

"Who was it?" Angela asked.

"I'm not sure. A man, deep voice. All he said was 'Tell Candace. Five rings,' before he hung up."

Marco felt a stirring of alarm, but he kept it from his face. “Let’s call Ridley at Coronado PD.”

Donna gave Brent a pat on the knee. “He and Brent are not the best of friends, but he did help get Sarah and Jett off that island. I’ll call. What should I tell him?”

“Did you say five rings?” Angela said, returning from the kitchen, her face grave.

JeanBeth eyed her. “Yes, what does it mean?”

“It’s a gang thing. I’ve counseled some young sailors who came from difficult backgrounds.” She toyed with the zipper on her jacket. “The rings is the number of phone calls you get before…” She looked at her mother and then at Candace. “It probably isn’t the time to talk about it.”

“Five rings before what?” JeanBeth repeated.

Angela grimaced. “Really, Mom. I shouldn’t have brought it up just now.”

“Angela,” JeanBeth said. “You have to tell us.”

All eyes were riveted on Angela. She pulled the patio door closed so Tracy would not hear from out in the yard.

“Five rings before what?” Marco asked.

“Five rings…” she cleared her throat, “before you’re dead.”

FOUR

It seemed to Candace that time sped up as soon as Angela dropped her bombshell. In a matter of three hours, an officer from the San Diego Police Department named Jennifer Barnes, and Ridley from the Coronado Police were meeting with the adults in the family room, while Lon and Tracy were occupied building a spaceship with Tracy's Lego set in the kitchen. Candace suspected Lon was silently taking in every word of the briefing, but fortunately, Tracy seemed oblivious.

Candace tried hard to focus, but her mind was still fogged in disbelief. The Pack had somehow tracked down her mother's phone number and called to inform Candace that she would be terrorized and killed for daring to testify against their gang brother Kevin Tooley. She wondered if the same message had been left on her own home phone. A shiver went through her. Though her mother and Angela flanked her on either side and Marco and Brent stood sentry nearby, Candace felt the roots of fear taking hold. Suddenly Marco's preparations did not seem so over-the-top.

"The district attorney has three witnesses that saw Kevin Tooley pull the trigger at the gas station," Barnes said. "So far you're the only one who has been threatened. I've been assigned along with Officer Ridley and another couple of San Diego officers to do drive-by checks of your house during the day and post a cop here at night until the trial."

Candace blinked. "But what about when I'm not at

home? Are you supposed to follow me for the next four weeks until our court date?"

Barnes shook her head. "I'm sorry, ma'am. We just don't have enough manpower for that. We'd like to suggest that you stay at home as much as possible."

"But I've got a daughter."

She nodded. "Any other kids?"

"Tracy is an only child." Only child, though Tracy desperately wanted a sibling. The words always hit Candace hard when she had to say them.

For a brief, shining period of time, she had carried that little sibling for Tracy. But then there was a knock on the door, the men in uniform respectfully reducing her life to ruins, and then there was the miscarriage when she'd lost the last part of Rick, and then there was a bottomless well of depression where she could see no hope, not even from the God she beseeched for mercy.

And then…

Angela's hand on her shoulder pulled her out of her reverie. How did her sister always know when Candace was teetering on the edge of that abyss? She covered her sister's fingers and squeezed back, telegraphing the thank-you she couldn't voice in front of the officers. How grateful she was to God for giving her sisters, who were truly the hands and feet of Jesus in her life. It felt doubly painful that she had not been able to give any siblings to Tracy. The only thing with which she could supply her daughter were the memories of her heroic father. Candace meant to preserve each one to keep Rick alive in Tracy's heart. What's more, she would not let her daughter see her fear. Her chin went up.

"Am I supposed to lock Tracy away for a month?"

Ridley tapped a pencil against his knee. "That's not Jay Rico's pattern. He usually orders the Pack to take out the direct threat to his organization and avoid collaterals."

"What does that mean?" Angela asked.

"They target the person who has crossed them," Marco said.

JeanBeth jerked. "But we're going to stop that, right?"

"Affirmative," Marco said. "There are enough of us to supplement the police watch. If the Pack is going to make a move, they'll have to get through us first."

"If?" Donna said. "So this could be intimidation only?"

Ridley nodded. "That's most likely. The Pack is not active here in Coronado, though we've been keeping our eye on some auto thefts, but it would be risky for them to take action. They are probably just trying to scare you."

They're doing a great job of that, Candace thought.

"The guy Rico sent to the college was more than intimidation," Marco said.

"Maybe." Ridley shrugged. "Could be he exceeded his orders from Rico."

"I'm not willing to put Candace's safety on the line for a maybe." Marco looked around at the family members. "From now on, she and Tracy stay inside unless it's urgent, and we get her whatever she needs, agreed?"

Everyone nodded.

"What about Tracy's school?" Candace said. Her daughter adored third grade and her teacher.

Marco shrugged. "You can get one of those home study packets, and she gets a vacation."

Candace felt like screaming. "So we're going to be prisoners until the trial is over?"

"Think of it as protective custody," Marco said.

"I feel like I'm being punished."

"Not punished, protected." Marco got up. "Let's talk about a schedule, and we need to know everything you have on Jay Rico."

They clustered together with phones and notepads, as if Candace was no longer even in the room.

Bullied. That's how she felt about this five rings business. Like she was back in junior high, being bullied by the boys who refused to let her take a seat on the bus. She remembered sitting on the sticky floor in the rear, trying to ignore the jeers from her classmates, wishing one person might make a space for her.

All she'd needed was a single brave soul to be her ally, but no one wanted to stand up to those bullies.

No one.

And Candace had resolved, after she got off at her stop on that long-ago day, never to be the subject of bullying again. The next day on the bus, she had elbowed her way to the front of the line, sitting down on the very first seat and announcing to the boys that she wasn't moving.

"And if you lay one finger on me," she'd shouted, "I will show you how I earned my black belt in karate." They'd believed her, even though she'd never set foot in a karate studio, and though they teased her relentlessly for the remainder of her school year, no one ever dared take her seat again.

Candace remembered how Rick had laughed in delight when she'd told him that story early in their marriage. "That's my girl," he'd said. "Don't ever let anyone bully you." He'd tossed an eighteen-month-old Tracy into the air until she'd giggled with delight. "And my baby girl is going to have her mama's tiger stripes, aren't you?"

And now here Candace was, a fully grown adult, being bullied by Jay Rico and his pack of thugs. Where were her tiger stripes now?

"I want to go home," she said quietly.

There was no response from the cluster of adults.

"I want to go home," she said louder.

Still no response. No one seemed to notice she'd said a word.

"It's not enough," Marco was saying. "I'm going to bring in some more guys if I can get them."

"Civilian help is dangerous," Ridley said.

"They aren't civilians, they're SEALs."

"This isn't their purview. They have no rights to act on domestic soil without orders."

Marco glared. "Try telling them that."

"I said," Candace called in a near shout, "I am going home right now."

They all turned to her. She realized at that moment that Tracy was standing in the doorway.

"Why are you yelling, Mommy?"

She plastered a smile on her face. "Because Mommy is tired, and it's time for us to go back to our own house."

Marco, her sisters and the two cops looked at her in surprise.

"If you could wait another hour or so…" Ridley suggested. "Until we get things in place…"

"Now," Candace said, in what she hoped was a calm, confident voice. "I am going back home now. With all of you looking out for us, I'm sure we'll be fine. Will someone give us a ride, or should I call a taxi?"

Candace sat in stony silence in the front seat of Marco's truck while Tracy prattled on in the back next to Bear. Marco had no idea what book Tracy was describing, something about a time-traveling pony, but he listened attentively and put in a "wow" once in a while at what he hoped were the appropriate times.

"And I'm gonna have a speaking part in the pioneer play we're doing just before Thanksgiving break. The practices are super fun. I know almost all my lines." She reached over to scratch Bear's tummy.

Anger edged up from Marco's stomach toward his chest when he considered that Tracy was going to miss out on the next few weeks of school. It was possible she wouldn't be in the show at all. No one had the right to strip away her childhood. When Jay Rico had sent his guy to interfere in Tracy's life, he had made himself Marco's enemy. Though he didn't know it yet, he would, and soon.

Marco realized he had the steering wheel in a death grip. He forced his fingers to relax. Clearing his throat, he shot a glance at Candace. "Got a guy coming tomorrow to watch your place."

She didn't answer.

"His name's Dev. You won't even know he's around."

"What about tonight?"

"That's me."

"Don't you think the cops are enough?"

"No."

"Why not? Because they aren't SEALs?"

He shrugged. *No, because they're not me, and no one cares about the two of you more than I do.* Again the out-of-the-blue thoughts kept sparking in his mind like tracer fire. "Dev and Lon are the best. They have skills that cops don't."

"Like what?" She closed her eyes. "Never mind, I don't want to know."

The strain in her voice was pronounced. On impulse he took her hand. "I know your independence is important to you. This is just for a while."

"But I…"

She looked in the rearview at Tracy, who was engrossed in singing a song.

"I feel like I'm being a coward, letting them win," Candace whispered.

She clutched his hand, her skin satin soft against his callused fist. "Rick said I should never hide from anything."

"You're sheltering in place, not hiding."

"But Rick…"

Marco squeezed her fingers. "Rick would want you safe. Period. Don't doubt that."

Tracy sat up. "Mommy, are you talking about Daddy?"

"Yes, honey. I was just saying that Daddy was a brave man."

"Because he fought for our country?"

"Yes, that, and because he always, always tried to do the right thing, even when it was hard."

The respect and adoration he heard in Candace's voice awakened something sad inside Marco. Had Gwen ever thought anything like that about him? As their marriage disintegrated, she'd seen him as her enemy, a man who thwarted her plans and desires, put her second after the navy. What would it be like to have a partnership based on deep respect like Rick and Candace had had? If he had a woman like Candace in his life, he'd spend every day making sure she knew how much he loved her.

Unsettled, he eased his hand from hers and she returned to her silent perusal of the quiet Coronado streets as they drove to her cottage.

Had he done wrong speaking out about Rick? Probably. Marco bit back a sigh. Another situation that called for a penknife and he'd used a machete. Typical.

He waved to the cop parked in front of the house, and directed Bear to stay in the truck. Marco walked them to the door, took the keys from Candace and unlocked it. He asked them to stay on the tiled entry of the house and did a quick perimeter check.

"Looks good," he said.

"What's going on?" Tracy demanded. "Why are you acting all weird?"

Candace knelt down to look in her eyes. "There are some bad people who don't want me to go to court. They are trying to scare me out of testifying."

Tracy twirled a strand of hair around her finger. "Are you scared, Mommy?"

"A little bit."

"Are you going to testify, anyway?"

"Yes."

Tracy nodded. "Good. I'm glad you're going to be brave..." She trotted toward the bedroom. "Like Unco."

Like Marco? She was supposed to say like her dad, like Rick.

Marco saw the discomfort on Candace's face and quickly looked away. What had he done to cause this? He didn't know, he wasn't sure, but now Candace was walking toward the kitchen.

"I'll see you in the morning," she said, voice strained.

"I..." *I'm sorry? I will fix it, somehow? I'll leave you two alone?* None of those things seemed like the right thing to say, especially since he had no intention of taking his eyes off them until the Jay Rico threat was neutralized.

Though he ached to walk to Candace and run his hands along her bowed shoulders, he was pretty sure that would make matters worse.

"I'll see you tomorrow," he mumbled. "Gonna be in the truck, and I'll set your alarm as I exit."

He did not hear her reply. A shadow outside caught his eye, moving quickly. Pulling back the partially opened curtain, he saw a figure sprint across the lawn, arm raised in a posture he'd seen before. He had only a moment to react before the kitchen window shattered with a thunderous crack.

FIVE

The explosion was so loud it paralyzed Candace, imprisoning her in a fetal position on the floor. Glass rained down but didn't touch her. Projectiles volleyed throughout the room. Bullets? She couldn't tell. She realized Marco had hurled himself over her, a shield against the glass that landed in jagged pieces all over, and whatever it was that was thunking around her, striking the floor so hard the vibrations jarred the tile. Marco's body jerked when the projectiles hit him, but he did not cry out or loosen his hold on her. There was a faint smell of smoke.

Tracy, was all she could think. *Run to Tracy. Get her out.*

But her body was still immobilized by fear and the echo of the deafening bang. Even if Marco wasn't holding her there she doubted she could move at all.

When the rain of debris subsided, Marco scooped her up and ran from the room. He carried her easily, making it to Tracy's door in moments. He shoved it open and brought her in, putting her on the bed next to Tracy, who sat bolt upright, eyes like round saucers.

"Mommy," she screamed.

"She's okay," Marco told Tracy. "Quiet now, half pint." He bent to look in Candace's face, smoothing the hair from her brow. His eyes took inventory, searching hers, gentle fingers skimming over her cheeks and neck. "Hurt?"

She shook her head, heart thundering, ears ringing. "You?"

"No." But she could see a welt forming on his forehead,

and another on his biceps where it showed through his torn sleeve. Dribbles of blood oozed from cuts on his forearms. "What…what was it?"

"Grenade." Marco looked at Tracy. "Take care of your mom. I'll be back."

"Where are you going? Stay here," Tracy said, the plea in her voice cutting into Candace as she threw her arms around her daughter.

Marco knelt next to the bed, his deep baritone soft as he took Tracy's hand, her small fist dwarfed in his. "Listen up, half pint." He smiled at her. "That was a lot of noise and fuss, but everything's okay and your mama isn't hurt. I've got to go check on the cop and make sure he's okay, too. Do you understand?"

Tracy clutched his fingers. "I don't want you to go. Please stay here with us."

"I will come back. I promise."

"But what if you don't?" Tracy said.

He looked at her gravely. "Do I keep my promises or not?"

"But…"

"No buts. Yes or no?"

"Yes, sir."

"That's right. I always keep my promises."

"'Cuz you're a SEAL?"

He grinned. "No, 'cuz that's the way God wants me to be. Being a SEAL just makes me extra cool."

It worked. Tracy offered a wobbly grin. He pressed a kiss to her head. "Lock the door behind me and sit tight."

Candace squeezed Tracy close after she'd clicked the flimsy door lock.

"What happened, Mommy?"

She strove for calm, matter-of-fact truth telling. "Someone threw something through our kitchen window."

"Why would they do that?"

"To scare me, I think." It was very effective. Her heart was hammering away at the speed of light.

"Because of the trial?"

"Yes."

"But you could have been hurt, or Unco," Tracy said, lips quivering again. Candace saw the beginnings of hysteria building there.

"No. No one is hurt, just like Marco said." She pulled her daughter into her lap. But Marco was right, she thought. She'd lambasted him for overreacting, for bringing in his SEAL friends, but he'd been absolutely correct. The Pack wasn't done terrorizing her, not by a long shot. They'd learned where she lived, and more importantly, where her daughter lived.

Candace went ice-cold. She tried to still the shaking in her hands as they waited minute by painful minute. It was taking far longer than she would have thought. What if the people who'd thrown the grenade were still there? Waiting for Marco to emerge? What if they'd taken out the cop?

No more death, she pleaded to God. *No more death to innocent people at the hands of these gangsters*.

The terror began to spread from her stomach into her limbs, icing her veins, inch by excruciating inch. She strained to hear something, but the silence continued and the minutes dragged on. Finally, she detected the wail of approaching sirens.

The doorknob rattled and Tracy screamed. "They got in the house. Mommy, they're coming to get us." Candace pushed Tracy behind her.

"It's Marco," called the loud voice from the other side. "Open up."

Candace's legs were shaking so badly she was grateful that Tracy leaped from the bed to let Marco in. She grabbed him around the waist.

"They didn't get you," Tracy sobbed.

"'Course not," he said, wiping her tears with the heel of his hand. "Came back, just like I promised."

Tracy sniffled.

He looked at her with mock severity. "Don't tell me you were worried?"

Tracy shrugged. "Just a little."

"I guess a little is okay. Pack two bags with whatever you'll need for a couple days," he said over her head to Candace. "We're leaving."

It was almost a relief. This was her home, but she did not want to cower every time someone drove past, the thunder of the grenade blast ringing in her memory. "Where are we going?"

"To talk to the cops, and then out of town."

Where? How? When will we be back? All the questions jammed up in her mind, stuck fast behind the fear. *Pack. Get your daughter out of here.*

The action of choosing several outfits, Tracy's markers and a drawing pad, and some basic toiletries calmed her. In a few more moments she'd packed her own tote, and Marco led them to the front of the house.

The officer they'd waved to on the way in was talking on the phone, while two others took pictures of the house and questioned the neighbors. Officer Ridley guided Tracy and Candace into the back of an ambulance, where a paramedic checked them over.

She tried to answer Ridley's questions, but knew ridiculously little about what had happened until Marco explained.

"It was a nonlethal grenade. They're used for crowd control, mostly. It detonates and shoots out rubber pellets that hit the target with blunt force."

Candace realized in that moment that thanks to Marco's quick thinking, he'd become the target instead of her. She could see now the purpling bruises forming on his arms and temple.

He waved away the paramedic's attention. "I'm fine." He turned to Ridley. "Don't like them being out in the open. If your questions are done, we're ready to go."

"Go where?" Ridley said.

Marco remained expressionless. "Somewhere safe."

"You need to tell us where that is. We're the police. We can protect them.

Marco shook his head. "You tried that. Rico's Pack is organized. They knew Candace would be at the college, and they know where JeanBeth lives and now Candace. This time we're doing it my way."

"No, we aren't," Ridley snapped. "You're a civilian. It's our job to protect them, not yours."

"You're right. I'm not bound by cop rules, so I can do whatever it takes."

"Sounds like you're talking about going vigilante, breaking the law."

Marco shook his head. "No, no law breaking unless it's absolutely necessary."

"That doesn't reassure me."

"And this doesn't reassure me," Marco said, waving an arm toward the broken kitchen window. "This could have gone very bad if that was a fragmentation grenade."

A fragmentation grenade? Candace didn't even want to know what sort of damage that might have done. The hairs on the back of her neck prickled. The two men were eyeing each other like angry bears.

"We'd like to go with Marco," she said to Ridley. "For now, I think that would be best."

Ridley was shaking his head, still staring Marco down. "We'll step it up. You do your part by staying out of the way."

He folded his arms across his muscled torso, his expression stone cold. "Sorry, but I'm not answering to you when it comes to the safety of my girls."

My girls? Was that how Marco saw them? Her initial flush of pleasure at the thought surprised her and awakened guilt right alongside. She and Tracy were Rick's girls. Always. She would not let any man take that away, not even Marco.

No time to worry about that now. There were more pressing matters at hand.

"We'd like to go now," Marco was saying.

Ridley started to answer when they heard a phone ringing from inside the house. Through the broken window they heard the answering machine pick up.

"Four rings," said the voice, before it cut off.

The breath was squeezed right out of her. Four more rings to go and she would be dead at Rico's hands.

Marco snaked an arm around her shoulders and gripped her tight.

"Like I said, they're on my watch now," he said, firing the challenge at Ridley.

She allowed the feel of Marco's strong palm to keep her from flying away into panic. She didn't want to rely on him, especially since his presence sent her feelings into a confusing spiral, but right at that moment she didn't see how she would make it without him.

My girls?

Later, she vowed. Later she would straighten out her relationship with Marco. Right now, she would do what was necessary to keep her daughter safe from Jay Rico and his gang of murderers.

SIX

Marco finally got Candace and Tracy into his truck and on the road. Tracy fell asleep almost immediately with her arm curled around Bear in the backseat. He rewound the tape in his memory.

My girls. He'd actually said that and noticed the startled flicker in Candace's eyes.

It's a mission, he reminded himself, *like all the others.* During the course of his career, he'd gone on too many missions to count, from counter narcotics operations in South America to dismantling enemy compounds in the Hamrin Mountains in Iraq. He'd stood side by side with brave men in sniper squadrons and assault teams, and his resolve to succeed and keep his military family safe had never wavered. The same determination flooded him now. That was it—resolve, nothing more.

He blinked back to the present at Candace's question. "Where are we headed?"

"To a beach house. Buddy of mine owns it."

"A beach house where?"

"Angel Vista, a village up the coast. North of Long Beach. Angela's coming, too, to help with Tracy. Brent and Donna are staying with your mom to run the office and keep an eye on her, since the first threat was delivered there."

"And how many SEALs will be joining us?"

He cocked an eyebrow at her. "How many would you guess?"

"I don't know, twenty?"

"Doesn't take twenty SEALs to get a job done."

"Oh, right," she said. "I forgot you are all invincible."

"I prefer to think of it as well trained and outrageously skilled."

She laughed and he was thrilled to hear it. It's what they needed to do, keep the conversation casual, light, away from his earlier remark in front of Ridley.

"Lon will stay and protect my mom?"

"Yes, and he's going to eat well, for sure."

Candace nodded thoughtfully, peeking behind her to check on the sleeping Tracy. "Marco," she said.

He knew what was coming and kept his gaze riveted out the front window. "Yes?"

"We love you, Tracy and I—you know that, don't you? I mean," she added quickly, "you've been amazing to us, through Dad's death and with my mom and sisters. All of the Gallaghers love you."

He nodded, breath held.

"But I need Tracy to remember Rick as her father and I need..." She twisted a finger in the hem of her shirt. "Well, that's just the way it is. Do you understand? I don't want her to be confused."

He nodded. "I did not mean to overstep. I'm going to take care of you, that's all I meant."

She seemed to relax a fraction. "Thank you."

Since he didn't want to deal with the pang of embarrassment, he focused on the road. *They aren't your girls, Quidel. Don't get it confused.* Candace was a spirited, stubborn, intelligent woman who needed him only for protection and nothing more.

So why did his skin prickle when her arm brushed against his? And what was the reason he wanted to run his fingers through her curly hair and feel the weight of it?

He blinked. *You had that once, remember?* Marco believed marriage was a forever commitment, and he'd had his one chance with the love of his life. It ended in disaster because he had failed Gwen.

But he wasn't going to fail Candace.

Checking the rearview for the dozenth time, he reassured himself that Rico's men had not followed them. There had been a car some three miles back, but nothing further.

His Bluetooth signaled a call.

"Chief."

"Retired, Dev. You can call me Marco."

"Once a chief, always a chief."

Marco smiled. "Got something for me?"

"Yes, sir. Waiting at the Party Palace to brief you."

"See you in ten."

"The Party Palace?" Candace said, when he disconnected. "Isn't it more like a safe house?"

"Dev has a keen wit."

"Keener than yours?"

"You always say I have no sense of humor whatsoever."

"Could be I'm wrong about you."

"Could be." He was pleased that she could still smile, even after the grenade incident. Candace Gallagher was an incredible woman.

They rolled up the steep drive and he noted the beach house was all but hidden from the road by a grove of enormous trees that had been left to grow without the benefit of trimming. It was a two-story structure, with a basement, and a covered garage so full of his buddy Pete's boats and Jet Skis that there was no way to get Marco's truck inside. He didn't see any sign of Dev's vehicle, but that did not surprise him. Dev rode a fast motorcycle and it was undoubtedly concealed somewhere nearby.

Tracy had awakened and she and Bear catapulted from the car.

"Where's the beach? Can we go find shells?"

He laughed. "Let's get you settled in right now, okay? We'll talk about the beach tomorrow when it's daylight."

Tracy raced Bear to the front door and Dev let them in. Marco introduced them. Tracy went wide-eyed at the sight of Dev, a tall African American with a monstrous beard and a set of shoulders almost as wide as Marco's.

He greeted them with hearty handshakes. "Nice to meet you, Ms. Gallagher and other Ms. Gallagher."

Tracy giggled.

Candace smiled. "You can call me Candace."

"Sure thing, Ms. Gallagher," he said, still grinning.

"I haven't had any luck, either," Angela said. "I've talked him down from Captain. Now he calls me Captain Ma'am."

Dev nodded, eyes shifting to Marco. "Chief, message from Ms. Donna Gallagher at the detective office."

"What is it?"

"DA needs to go over Ms. Gallagher's testimony Monday at ten. He'll be at the county courthouse in Long Beach."

"All right," Marco said. "Thoughts?"

"You lead, I'll follow and check for tails."

"Recon?"

"Conference room is on the ground floor, six exits. Metal detectors and security checkpoint in the lobby."

"Got all that already?"

He shrugged. "I'm good. What can I say?"

"Don't let it go to your head. Tracy?"

"Will stay put with Captain Ma'am. Coastie's arriving soon. Can he handle himself?"

Marco recalled how Brent had survived a beating and a hostile surf that would have killed most men, long enough to save his sister's life and probably Donna's. "Yeah, he can handle himself."

"I'll put him on a radio."

"And Angela can take care of herself, too. She's navy, after all," Marco said.

Angela sighed. "A chaplain, but I had the obligatory combat training. I'm probably best at calling for help."

"Don't let her fool you, Dev. All the Gallagher sisters are made of tough stuff."

"I don't doubt it, Chief. They put up with you, after all."

"Funny," Marco said, as Candace and Angela laughed.

"What's the code name for Ms. Gallagher?" Dev said.

"It should be Gumdrop," Angela said promptly. "That was her nickname as a kid."

Candace groaned. "You know how many years it took to get everyone to forget that nickname?"

"Gumdrop," Dev said. "Got it."

Candace glared at her sister.

"It's better than mine," Angela said. "Behind my back, they called me Giraffe when I was deployed. Something about my height."

"Gonna tell them your nickname, Chief?" Dev said, eyes sparkling with mischief.

"Negative, and if you'd like to keep breathing, you won't, either."

Dev laughed. "You're the boss."

To preempt the question from coming out of Candace's mouth, Marco said, "How about I cook up some spaghetti for dinner? I have some supplies in the truck."

"Men who can cook, not bad," Candace said. "We'll go set the table." She shot him a sly look. "But don't think I'm going to forget about that nickname. I'll get it out of Dev yet."

"You'll get no such intel from me." Dev zipped his lips, turned an imaginary key and mimed throwing it away before he departed to the kitchen.

Marco watched them go. As he headed for his truck, he tried to breathe away the tension. Candace was safe for the moment, secured in a place where no one could get the jump on them. JeanBeth was under watch and he'd trust Dev and Lon to meet any kind of threat that Rico could toss at them.

So why did he have the tingling feeling, deep down in his gut, that something was about to go very wrong?

Candace helped Dev with the dishes while Marco did a check of the exterior of the old beach house. When the last dish was dried and put away in the worn wooden cupboards, Dev gave her a sweeping bow and disappeared somewhere. He and Marco would be bunking on sofas in the small downstairs room connected to a dark-paneled den that smelled of old cigars.

Candace, Angela and Tracy would be installed in the bedrooms upstairs, complete with a tiny bathroom and shower where Angela had just taken Tracy for her bedtime preparations.

Candace sighed. She would have to break the news to Tracy very soon that she would not be returning to school for a while. She didn't look forward to the upset that would ensue. *Thank you, Jay Rico, the man responsible for turning our lives upside down.*

Fuming, she paced around the living room, perusing dusty bookshelves that held information on every kind of boat imaginable, plus a stack of tattered sailing magazines, while she formulated a plan of her own. She wasn't about to sit around waiting for her sisters and Marco to figure out how to bring down Jay Rico. As long as she had her laptop, she was fully capable of doing some of her own sleuthing. Pulling a plaid-cushioned chair up to the sturdy table, she began firing up her computer just as Marco came in.

"Working?" he asked.

"Just starting."

"Goal?"

"I want to know more about Kevin Tooley."

"Our jailed gas station shooter?" He raised an eyebrow. "Thought our focus was Rico."

"Rico's interest in keeping Tooley out of prison seems unusual to me."

Marco sat next to her, arms folded across the tabletop. "Not to me—he's a ruthless thug protecting his interests. But I trust your instincts."

She felt her cheeks warm at the compliment. "Thank you."

"So tell me what you're thinking."

"Rico's people have been jailed before. One has been in prison for six years. There's no evidence that I can see that Rico started a campaign of terror to keep any of his other gang family out of prison, yet he's heavily invested in Kevin Tooley. Don't you find that strange?"

Marco lifted a shoulder. "Maybe, but I don't think he's the most rational guy. He uses intimidation and coercion when he feels the need."

"Sure, in more important situations. But why in this case? Kevin Tooley is a kid, only eighteen, so he's obviously not in a position of power in the Pack. Why go to all the trouble to prevent me from testifying against a young kid?

Marco was silent, staring at her, considering. He was weighing her reasons with calm deliberation and the respect gave her confidence to continue. "I want to understand more about Tooley, something to explain why Rico's interested in this case."

He nodded. "Okay. I'll leave the 'why' to you. I'm more concerned with how he intends to go about stopping your testimony."

"It's not just mine. There are two other witnesses, remember?"

Dev knocked on the door frame with a knuckle. His face was grave and Angela stood next to him.

"Just got some bad news," she said.

Marco straightened. "Let's hear it."

Candace steeled herself for whatever was going to come next.

"Donna heard from Barnes that one of the other witnesses has disappeared," she said. "They've got people out looking, but they think he might have gotten a message from Rico and decided to get out of Dodge."

Dev rubbed a hand over his thick beard. "Seems like it's down to one other witness and Gumdrop."

And then there were two...

Candace fought down the shiver of fear. She would not let him win.

"All right," she said, forcing her chin high and trying to show her tiger stripes. "So be it."

SEVEN

Tracy weathered the disappointment of missing church on Sunday with only a minor upset, but when Candace finally had the courage to tell her on Monday morning she would have to skip school for the foreseeable future, the child dissolved into a puddle of tears that wrenched Marco's heart.

"Why can't you just find the bad guys, Unco?" she wailed. "I'm gonna miss the play practice today, and tomorrow is library."

"I am going to find them, kiddo," he said. "I promise."

She was only mildly placated by an early morning walk to the beach with Marco, Bear and Candace, where they searched for shells along the quiet stretch of sand. In her enthusiasm, Candace wandered close to the foamy edge of the water, her back to the pristine Pacific, jeans rolled up to her calves. She looked no more than a young girl herself, her laughter carrying over the sound of the surf.

A big wave, powered by the fall breeze, rolled in behind Candace, poised to douse her. Without thinking, Marco took her by the waist and twirled her away from the reach of the salt water. She grabbed his shoulders to keep her balance and clung to him, bringing her so close he could smell the subtle fragrance she always wore, the heady scents of vanilla and cinnamon.

Her curls tickled his face and he reached out to smooth them down. She was close, so close, brown eyes wide and heavily lashed, lips parted and cheeks flushed. He was overwhelmed by a desire to kiss her. The ocean crashed around them and his emotions did the same inside. She lingered there, close, and he wondered if she felt any of the same longing that kept him immobilized in that spot of sand, his arms clasping her to him. She tipped her mouth upward, the tiniest fraction of an inch nearer, and he was drawn as if by a powerful tide to close the gap, until she took a breath and stepped away.

"Thanks," she said, tucking some hair behind her ear. "I don't have enough extra clothes to get these wet."

"Uh, sure."

He fisted his hands on his hips, trying to breathe some sense back into his brain. She gazed out at the rolling surf and he stood there like a big, dumb block of stone, unsure what to say.

Had he really been about to kiss her? His own lack of control disturbed him.

"Come on, Unco," Tracy called against the wind. "There are some cool shells over here."

Relieved, he joined Tracy and Bear, scouring the beach and trying to leave his inexplicable behavior behind him.

Candace joined them, seemingly unruffled.

He found a perfect sand dollar, gingerly extracting it from the sand and handing it to Tracy with all the solemnity of a king bestowing a royal favor.

She took it, wide-eyed. "It's not even chipped or anything. I'm gonna put it in my jar with the shells Daddy found me." She continued, kneeling now, to search out more treasures tossed up by the sea.

Candace pushed the hair from her face as she joined them. "Rick took her to the beach just before he deployed for the last time. She was only two, so she doesn't remember, but he found some beautiful shells and put them in a jar for her."

"That was real nice."

She knelt next to Tracy. "Baby, I know you don't remember, but Daddy said you were the best shell finder in all of California."

Marco saw moisture sparkling against Candace's lashes.

"When we get home, I will show you a picture of you two at that beach, okay?"

"Okay, Mommy." Tracy put the shell in her pocket and raced with Bear down the sand.

Candace continued to stare after the two. "I keep reminding her, but they're my memories, not hers."

The words rang with sadness, making Marco feel even more of a heel for his earlier impulse to kiss her. "I'm sorry."

"He was a great dad. He never was the kind to 'take her to play,' he always played right along. First in the ball pit, the water, the 'tiny tot' days at the park. He would sure have loved doing these things with her now."

The things that Marco was doing, making memories with another man's child. And suddenly he was infringing again, inserting himself where Candace clearly did not want him to be. How would he feel if his child had no memories of her father? If all that love and devotion had been erased from a kid's life by a roadside IED? But it wasn't all erased, not as long as Candace was around to keep Rick's memory alive for his little girl.

Marco walked away a few paces and left them to their treasure hunt, Candace, Tracy and the missing spot where Rick should be.

On their way back to the house to prepare for their courthouse visit, Marco made sure to hang back a pace. The waves rolled in and out, their ceaseless rhythm scouring away any trace of a human presence.

Keep the distance, he reminded himself, *and everything will be just fine.*

Candace dressed in slacks and the nicest blouse she'd packed, and restored her beach-blown hair to order. The prickling in her nerves was not due to the courthouse visit—she felt completely secure with Marco and Dev's security measures—but with what had happened on the beach. Her mind was under control; Marco was a friend, protecting and helping. But her feelings were another matter.

Something inside her had wanted to lean forward and receive what she imagined might have been a kiss from Marco. But that could not be, Candace told herself sternly. What was she doing, thinking about kissing another man, any man? Especially in light of the obvious problem that Tracy did not remember her father?

But I can fix that, Candace thought, throwing up a prayer to God. *Please don't let Rick vanish from Tracy's life like he vanished from mine.* And as for thoughts of kissing Marco, those would be banished from both her mind and her emotions.

Bolstered, she kissed Tracy and Angela. Brent arrived and met Dev, who offered a handshake. "Heard you were a puddle jumper."

"Rescue swimmer," Brent said, quirking a smile.

"You any good?" Dev inquired.

Brent laughed. "Next time you're drowning in twenty-foot seas, I'll rappel out of a helicopter and show you just how good I am."

Dev gave him a respectful grin. "All right, then. Hold down the fort, Coastie."

"I will, and you drive safely, okay? No falling off your motorcycle or anything."

When the bantering was finished, Marco got into the truck and they drove away toward the county courthouse. Candace didn't see where Dev had gone, but she knew he was there somewhere, watching.

Like Rico's men?

Marco was silent for the whole trip, probably just as

well. She'd make it clear that she didn't want any deeper connection with him than she already had, and didn't want Tracy to bond with him any more than she'd already done.

Candace thought of Tracy's joy when she spent time with Marco, and her stomach pinched with guilt. She recalled the school plays he'd attended and even a classroom tea, cramming his giant body into a first-grade-sized chair. Every year for her birthday he carved her a tiny wooden bunny to add to her collection, a reminder of an orphaned rabbit they'd tried to save. Was it wrong to put distance between Tracy and a man she loved? But it was not right to allow Rick to be replaced in her heart or Tracy's.

Candace clasped her hands together and prayed, once again, for God to help her be both mother and father to her daughter. Relaxed, she drifted off until the slowing of the truck roused her. "I didn't know I was that tired."

Marco got out to open the door for her, but she hopped out first. She meant to say thank you, but he was propelling her toward the courthouse, his hand on her back.

They passed through the metal detectors and Candace had her purse searched. The precautions were comforting. There was no way Jay Rico would try anything in a heavily secured government building, and besides, he had no way of knowing she was here.

After forty-five minutes of waiting in a small conference room, during which Marco sat still as a statue and Candace paced, checked her phone, drank some water and paced some more, a sturdy woman with a neat bun entered.

"I'm Mandy Livingston, assistant to the district attorney. I'm sorry, but he's still in court, so I don't think he can meet with you today. But we can go over the particulars, okay?" She shot a look at Marco. "Would you mind waiting outside, sir?"

He hesitated, and Candace thought he might resist, but she nodded at him.

"I'll be right outside the door."

Livingston started in and Candace was again lost in that horrible time four months before, reliving the shooting, the cold expression on Kevin Tooley's face as he aimed his gun out the car window and murdered a young man at the gas station.

"Why did he do it?" she blurted.

Livingston looked surprised. "Tooley?" She paused. "From what we can gather from our snitches, the victim threatened to go to the police with information about a car Tooley stole."

"What do you know about Tooley's background?"

She cocked her head. "Why is this of interest?"

"I'm not sure."

"Okay. Here are the bare-bones facts. He was born in Los Angeles to a single mom, Yolanda Tooley, who was a receptionist at a gym. She was struck by a car and killed when Kevin was three. It was a hit-and-run and the driver was never caught. Kevin was raised by various people, an uncle notably. Started seeking out the gang life at age twelve."

Twelve. Only a little older than Tracy.

"Minor trouble with the law and then fast forward to age eighteen, when he killed Jack Matthews at the gas station." Livingston closed her notebook. "I've got to get back to court. We'll be in touch."

"Ms. Livingston," Candace said. "The other witness, the one who disappeared. Any success tracking him down?"

"No, I'm afraid not, but the remaining witness is in protective custody." She paused. "You should be also, to be blunt."

I am, she wanted to say, but the woman was already gone. When Marco stuck his head in, the exhaustion of reliving the whole episode crashed in on her and she found she barely had the energy to rise from the chair.

Marco handed her a paper cup. An enticing aroma drifted from under the lid.

"Vanilla latte," he said.

She goggled. "This from the man who tells me that coffee with vanilla isn't really coffee."

Marco shrugged. "Figured you'd need a little pick-me-up, and there was a coffee kiosk near the conference room."

With a sigh of contentment she sipped her drink while he checked in with Dev.

"All clear," Dev said.

Suitably revived, Candace followed Marco out, leaving him for a moment to head to the ladies' room.

Three women were washing their hands and the stalls were all occupied, so she took her place in line, wondering why men never seemed to have to wait. Behind her, a bored young blonde with heavy eyeliner, smelling of cigarettes, was checking her phone. She bumped Candace with her elbow.

"Sorry," she mumbled.

"No problem."

When Candace emerged from the stall, the bathroom was empty except for the blonde girl who lounged against the wall. She was no longer immersed in her phone, but staring straight at Candace.

There was no friendliness in her smile, and her dark eyes were flat and cold. Candace's breath crystallized in her lungs as the woman leaned forward.

"Jay Rico is looking forward to meeting you," she whispered, reaching for Candace's throat.

Instead of shrinking back as her instincts demanded, Candace grabbed the hair spray she happened to have in her purse and pressed the nozzle. It wasn't as effective as the pepper spray she hadn't been allowed to carry into the building, but it was enough.

The blonde out, pawing at her eyes, which had gone red from the chemicals.

"Tell Mr. Rico I'd love to meet him," Candace said.

The girl turned and slammed out of the bathroom.

EIGHT

Candace started after her, but Marco must have read the situation, because he was already in pursuit down the hall-way.

"Stop!" he cried.

The girl took off for the stairs, dodging around court-house visitors.

He grabbed his radio. "Dev, girl in the south stairwell, maybe twenty, blond hair, eye trouble."

Candace heard Dev click the radio button to confirm.

Marco jogged to the top of the stairs, but had to stop when a flood of people emerged from a conference room into the hall. With a look of profound irritation, he returned to Candace's side.

"What happened?" he asked.

"The woman told me Jay Rico was looking forward to meeting me."

His teeth clamped shut with an audible click. "She didn't hurt you?"

"She bumped me with her bag, but when she went for my throat I blasted her with my hair spray." Candace was still breathing hard from the encounter, but she wasn't teary or shaking, much to her surprise.

He grinned. "Smart thinking."

"Just reacting. I'm not sure how I thought of it." She blew out a shuddering breath.

Marco went to put his arm around her shoulders, but she waved him away. "I'm okay. Let's go."

They went out the front, nice and public, plenty of people around on a midmorning Monday. The crush of strangers did not ease Candace's mind when she considered that Rico's lady friend had strolled right up to her in a public bathroom. If she wasn't safe in a courthouse, where in the world would she be protected from the Pack?

He got her in the truck, and Dev radioed.

"She didn't exit. Must've gone back into the building. I'm en route to check the other stairwell and alert the security people."

"I just called Donna at the office," Marco said. "Going to drive for a while. Too risky to return to the Party Palace in case Rico's got eyes on us."

Dev clicked off.

Candace was glad to be driving, moving, anything to give her time to think over what had happened. Not what, she realized. How? How had they known when and where she would be? As cars passed, she peered into each one, looking for malicious expressions, signs of unusual interest. If this situation wasn't resolved soon, she would become downright paranoid. She wondered how Marco had made the transition from active duty, where he was constantly a target, to a civilian, without falling victim to that very paranoia. Another reason to respect the men and women who faced life and death, and then an uncomfortable transition back into everyday living.

Marco had turned down a quiet road that would take them to the freeway. She allowed her body to relax a fraction. Then she noticed his gaze riveted to the rearview mirror as a car pulled in behind his truck.

Dark paint, tinted windows. Her throat grew dry. Paranoia again?

The driver closed the gap, now only a few feet from their own vehicle. She clutched the armrest. "It's them."

"Dev..." Marco started to say into the radio, just as their pursuer sped up and rammed the truck.

Candace screamed. The hard impact sent the radio flying out of Marco's grip and onto the floor.

He accelerated, putting some precious distance between them. The freeway on-ramp was around the next corner, past a sunken grassy lot. Once they were on the freeway, they would be safe, she thought, surrounded by the constant flood of Southern California traffic. She leaned forward as if to try and lend speed to Marco's truck. His efforts paid off as they began to pull away.

He punched the accelerator harder.

"We're going to make it," she thought with a thrill.

Without warning a second car pulled out in front—an Escalade with more tinted glass.

With no choice, Marco slammed the brakes, sending the truck into a skid that carried them over the shoulder and down to the grassy lot below. Only the seat belt kept her from being thrown around the cab of the truck.

"Get the radio," he said, over the mad bumping of the tires.

She tried to reach down for it, but the truck was bucking over the uneven ground and it was all she could do to keep from smashing her head on the console.

"Hold on," he shouted, as the vehicles closed in on them, front and back.

Part of Candace felt strangely detached as she thought logically over the situation. Their ambush had been strategic, and well planned. There was no other traffic on this road. She realized this must have been the Pack's plan all along. The girl was probably ordered there to scare her into leaving the safety of the courthouse. They'd been watching, waiting, and biding their time to spring this trap. There was little hope that any passersby would notice the attack, since the sharp dip of the landscape shielded them from any prying eyes.

The cars pulled to a stop, and Marco had no choice but to do the same.

He left the engine running and unbuckled his seat belt. He shoved the KA-BAR knife into his waistband before turning to her.

"Stay in the truck with the doors locked and your head down. Radio or call Dev as soon as you can," he said. "When you see a chance, hit the gas and get back to the road."

Her pulse slammed against her throat and her hands had gone cold. "What are you going to do?"

"Meet Jay Rico."

She gasped, scared by the hard glint in Marco's eyes, which were always gentle when they looked at her. It was as if he was two men, and the soldier had stepped out in front of the kind man she knew. "Marco, you can't. Stay here. I'll call the cops." She clutched his arm. "Please do not do this."

He put his big palm over hers. "Gonna be okay."

"How is this going to be okay?" she hissed. "This is the furthest thing from okay."

His mouth twisted in a small grin. "Good guys always win, remember?"

No, they don't, she wanted to scream. *Rick didn't. My father didn't, and I don't want you to die, too.*

Through the rear window, she saw two young men in baggy jeans approaching the truck. There had been no movement from the forward Escalade.

"Let's try to get away together," she said, frantically reaching for him.

"Go when you can," Marco repeated, and then he got out of the truck, slamming the door behind him.

The two men approaching suddenly froze. The taller one was Shoe Guy from the junior college parking lot. His eyes narrowed into slits of hatred.

"Got some new shoes, I see," Marco said cheerfully. "Very nice"

"Shut your mouth, man."

"'Course, they're not as nice as the one my dog chewed up, but I guess you had to get this pair on the cheap, huh? Shopped the sales? Maybe you should ask Rico to up your footwear allowance."

The guy dived at him, bat in hand, and Marco easily sidestepped, sending him crashing to the ground.

He got to his feet, discarding the bat and drawing a knife from his belt. "Okay, smart mouth. Let's see what you got."

"I thought you already saw that. How's the wrist? Tender?" He saw the bruise where he'd hit him with the plank in the parking lot. Marco watched, hands loose and ready. He'd had hours upon hours of combat training, enough to keep his cool when things went south. Shoe Guy was mad, his face tight and pinched, and that gave Marco the advantage. Mad combined with insufficient training made you sloppy. Mistake number one. *Bring it on, kid. I'm ready for a rematch.*

Shoe Guy was considering his options on where to cut Marco first. Mistake number two. Hesitation gave your opponent the power. Marco struck out with a quick punch to the throat that sent him to the ground, gagging.

His companion retreated a couple steps.

Marco heard the sound of clapping and allowed a quick look.

A guy in his late thirties, with hair slicked back in a dark braid, leaned against the back bumper of the Escalade, his eyes concealed by mirrored sunglasses. He wore loose-fitting jeans, scuffed leather boots and a button-up shirt, slightly rumpled. Marco recognized him from his internet search as Jay Rico.

"Points for you, Popeye," Rico said. "Or does everybody call you Chief?"

Marco kept guy number two in his peripheral vision. He could disable him easily also, he figured, until the man pulled a pistol from his belt. That complicated things. He'd probably still be able to disarm him, but wasn't going to risk any stray bullets striking Candace. He wondered if she'd found the radio.

Hit the gas and get out of here, Candace, he silently willed. *What are you waiting for?*

"Come on over," Rico said, gesturing. "I hear you've been asking around about me." His voice was soft, slightly high pitched. He reminded Marco of the guy who made his kale smoothies back in Coronado, a wiry type who worked real hard to appear relaxed and easygoing.

Marco moved closer, feeling the dude with the gun shadowing him from behind. The Escalade's driver got out, too, a gun in his hand. His hair was greasy, same baggy clothing and his front tooth was missing. Would it kill any of these guys to pull their pants up? The count stood at three, not including the one still gagging on the ground. Two guns and probably more, since Rico was undoubtedly carrying a weapon, as well.

When Marco got within a couple feet of Rico, the gangster held up a palm. "All right. You wanted to talk to me, so here I am." He patted a hand to his breast pocket and shook his head. "Trying to quit smoking, but man, that nicotine has a hold on me. Never start, that's what I tell my boys. Cigarettes will kill you."

Marco wasn't good at small talk and at the moment his desire to make idle chitchat with a gang boss was zilch. "Stay away from Candace Gallagher."

Jay cocked his head slightly and took off the sunglasses. His eyes were the color of midnight, glinting with curiosity more than malice. Didn't fool Marco. He'd read the case files on Rico, who had allegedly gunned down a convenience store owner when he was sixteen. The owner's wife had been too scared to testify. That was just the first of a list of crimes.

"No getting acquainted, I see," Rico said.

"I know all I need to know about you."

"Really? That's arrogant, isn't it?" Rico shook his head in disgust. "You come barreling into town, think you can call the shots regarding my family without even understanding who you're up against? Without giving your opponent the proper consideration? What's the matter with you?"

"Situation's black-and-white. One of your 'family' gunned down a kid at a gas station. Kevin Tooley's going to prison. End of story."

"It's not the end of my story." Rico leaned back on the bumper as if he were a king on a throne. "I write my own scenes the way I want them to be. I got the power to do that, you see?"

"You control everything, huh?"

"Oh, yeah. In my neighborhood, I do."

"This isn't your neighborhood, and that's not the way it's going to work this time. Tooley's going to prison."

"I don't think so. Fuzz is just a kid, too young to do hard time." Rico's lip curled in a small smile. "We call him Fuzz on account of he can't even grow a beard." The driver crimped a smile and they shared a chuckle.

"Eighteen," Marco said. "Legal adult. Old enough to know better than to shoot people."

Rico lifted a shoulder. "A mistake."

"One he's going to pay for."

There was several seconds of silence before Rico folded his arms across his chest, something in his face turning to steel. "You don't get to decide that for my family. He's Pack. Untouchable."

"And you call *me* arrogant."

Rico cracked a smile that didn't reach his eyes. "Funny man. You should do stand-up."

"Bottom line is you're not going to hurt my family to protect yours."

Rico straightened and walked to Marco. He was a few inches shorter and had a slighter physique, but he was strong, his forearms knotted with muscle, a scar twisting along his right wrist along with the tattoos. Gym rat, Marco suspected. He stared and Marco stared right back into those black eyes. It was like looking at a long stretch of bad road.

"On that we agree. Family is everything, isn't it?" Rico said softly. "You were a SEAL. You understand duty and commitment to your people. You would give your life for your men. We're not so different."

"If my guys were murdering criminals," he said calmly, "I'd let them take their punishment."

Some emotion glimmered in the dark pools of Rico's eyes. "Yeah?" he said softly. "What if they were addicts?"

Marco's gut lurched in surprise, but he kept his face stony. Rico had done his research on his adversary, just as Marco had.

"So if your girl was a heroin addict, I wonder, would you help her out, or go be the big, bad navy SEAL and turn your back?" Rico was watching for any sign that his bullet had hit the target. Marco wouldn't give him one, even though his stomach was churning.

"Naw," Rico said with a shake of his head. "I guess you would put your family first, right? Stay home and help your girl get past the addiction?" He stopped as if remembering. "Oh, wait a minute. You didn't, did you? You left her to go do your Popeye thing, and she crashed hard. Divorced you, I heard, messed herself up real bad and never did get clean. Died, didn't she?"

After she'd spiraled downward into destruction, endured a string of failed relationships and stints in jail, he'd finally lost track of Gwen for good until he got word the past December that she'd died of an overdose. Hurt took him to his knees then, pain so bad only prayer saved him from tortured memories that came back again in hideous Technicolor.

If he'd taken a different approach…

If he'd tried harder…

If he hadn't left her alone in strange places while he pursued his navy career…

He gritted his teeth and, with all the effort he could muster, kept his voice level. "Stay away from Candace Gallagher."

They were almost nose to nose. "Not going to put my boy Fuzz in prison."

"He's guilty. He's gonna do the time."

Rico jutted out his chin. "Here's the scenario. If Candace Gallagher tries to testify, then she's going to die."

"You first," Marco said.

"So it's gonna be like that, huh?"

Marco saw Rico's driver step forward, gun in his hand. He got ready to dive for the guy. "Yeah, it's gonna be like that."

Rico waved the driver off, taking his own gun from his waistband.

"Then let the games begin." Without warning, he swiveled his arm and shot five rounds into the windshield of Marco's truck.

NINE

Candace already had her foot on the gas when she saw Rico reach for the gun tucked in his waistband. Anger flamed up hot and hungry in her soul. There was no way she was going to allow Marco to be gunned down right in front of her eyes.

When the bullets exploded through the windshield, adrenaline fueled her in time to pull herself down below the dash. Somehow she managed not to scream. Unable to see where she was going, she jammed her foot to the accelerator.

The truck hurtled in the direction of the Escalade. She cringed, praying she wouldn't plow over Marco. The vehicle flew forward, and she tried to estimate the distance before contact. She figured she had another couple feet before the fender impacted Rico's car.

Wrong. The suddenness of the crash slammed her against the steering wheel, driving the breath out of her in a whoosh of air. She tried to open the driver's door, but it refused to budge, so she scrambled to the passenger side. Throwing it open, she saw she'd crumpled the front end of the Escalade and ruined the front end of Marco's truck.

The man whom she suspected was the driver sat upright on the ground, dazed, blood trickling from his lips from a spot where his tooth was missing. There was no sign of Marco or Rico.

Frantically, she looked under the Escalade and the truck, praying she wouldn't find Marco's mangled body in the wreck. Keeping close to the shelter of the open door, she strained to see any sign of Marco.

Arms went around her from behind. She screamed and struggled, but Jay Rico lifted her and carried her away from the wreck to the undamaged SUV that had closed them in from the rear. She pummeled him with her fists and even pulled his hair, but couldn't dislodge herself. He shoved her inside.

She kicked out, catching him in the knee.

He stopped and, to her great surprise, grinned at her. "You remind me of a woman I knew. Spirited and feisty. 'No one owns me, Rico,' she would say." His smile faded and something sharp and cold took its place. "But she betrayed me. I decided a long time ago that no one gets to do that, so I didn't have a choice. You gotta draw the battle lines in your life, you know?" A look of contemplation flickered across his delicate features.

"I've drawn mine," she said shakily. "You won't scare me off."

"Okay," he said, pulling his gun and putting it to her temple. "Then you get to die now."

She wanted to scream, but nothing would come out of her mouth. The only thing her brain could recognize was that cold circle of metal where the gun pressed against her skull.

A body slammed into Rico from behind. His chin impacted the metal door frame, and the gun spiraled away. Marco, eyes blazing, threw Rico to the ground and stood facing him, hands fisted. Rico lay on his back, swiping at his bloody face.

Candace tumbled from the car and fell to her knees. Dev appeared, helping her up, and through her tangle of hair she saw Marco closing in on Jay Rico.

Rico got to his feet in a blaze of hatred.

"I will kill you both," he growled. "And you will be forced to watch her die first, Popeye."

"Not gonna happen," Marco snarled back.

Rico's cohort gunned the SUV to life. The dazed Escalade driver dived into the backseat with Shoe Guy. One of them shoved the rear door open and Marco dropped to the ground as a spray of automatic weapon fire whizzed through the air. Bullets furrowed the dirt as he rolled under the truck for cover. He caught a glimpse of Rico jumping into the passenger seat before the car careened away. Striking his fists on the ground in frustration did nothing to let his anger out. Rico had escaped, again, and almost murdered Candace. Again.

He got to his feet and found Candace behind the truck, where Dev had taken her for cover when the shots started.

She flew to him and wrapped him in a hug. "I'm so glad I didn't run you over."

"Me, too." He held her close, allowing his mouth to stray to her neck, feeling the frantic beating of her pulse against his lips. He pressed his face to her skin and breathed in the scent of her. She was unharmed, unhurt in spite of his failure to read the situation. *Thank You, Lord.*

He shot Dev a look as she slipped from his grasp and pulled her jacket sleeves over her hands, as if she could somehow hide herself.

"What took you so long to get here?" he said to Dev.

"Traffic, man. It's ridiculous in SoCal."

Candace laughed. The fact that she could actually find humor at the moment took Marco's breath away. He examined his truck.

"It's drivable," he said. "Going to..." He tried to resist the urge to bark orders. "I suggest we go to the office, wait until dark to return to the safe house." The whine of sirens sounded in the distance. "After we talk to the cops, I mean. This is going to be a fun conversation."

"I'm not into chatting with cops. It gives me a headache," Dev said, jutting his chin.

He walked away toward his parked motorcycle, before the cops arrived.

Marco and Candace endured what turned into a two-hour interview that concluded at the Long Beach Police station. He was just grateful that Ridley and Barnes had not arrived to make the situation even more unpleasant. It was almost one o'clock by the time they were released, though Marco's truck had been impounded for evidence. Marco led Candace to his motorcycle, which was parked in the police lot.

"How did that get here?" she asked.

"Lon brought it."

Marco put his spare helmet over her curls. She looked all of twenty with the helmet accentuating her freckles and curly tendrils of hair peeking out.

"And it's a good idea to keep switching up the vehicles," he added.

"In case the Pack tries something else?"

"Yeah." He fastened the buckle for her, fingers grazing the silk of her cheeks. He wanted to pull her close, but steeled himself and kept his distance. After a calming breath, he asked in the nicest way he knew how, "Why didn't you drive away like I told you to? You should have gotten clear. That was the first priority."

"Yeah, I know," she said with a sigh. "But I'm not great at the following-orders thing."

He fought hard against a smile. "Color me shocked."

She sniffed. "Besides, you needed help."

"I had it under control." Brash words, and he was not surprised when she saw right through them.

"Uh-huh. Sure you did."

"Things would have turned around. I was sizing up the situation when you made your move."

"Right."

Candace had always had the power to read his thoughts,

his heart. He couldn't bluff with her, never had been able to. He huffed out a breath and confessed, "I didn't read the situation right. I should never have allowed this to happen." He found himself looking at his boots, the ground, the long afternoon shadows playing across the grass, anywhere but her face.

She hooked a finger under his chin and guided his gaze until it locked on hers—chocolate splendor, rich and sweet.

"Marco," she said, "quit it."

"Quit what?"

"Blaming yourself. I'm safe because of you and Dev. Tracy is safe back home and—" she gave him grin "—let's face it, you're safe because I saved your bacon."

He couldn't hold back his chuckle at her cockiness. "You are too much, Candace Gallagher."

"I know, so what do you say we go to the office and find out how to make some trouble for Jay Rico? He's made plenty for us already."

Marco grinned. How he loved that streak of sass in her. "Yes, ma'am."

They climbed aboard Marco's motorcycle. She clung tight to his waist, her chin pressed against his shoulder blade. Her bravado aside, it didn't change the truth. As much as he wanted to let his conscience be soothed, he replayed the scenario over and over, how close they'd come to disaster on his watch.

Rico was not just a dumb thug. The guy had smarts and he was absolutely convinced he was in the right. Deadly combination. Marco allowed his brain to replay their conversation. Rico had accused him of something he'd blamed himself of many times—deserting Gwen for his duty.

But hadn't he tried everything? Deployed thinking she had beaten her addiction? Maybe that was self-delusion. He'd chosen to see what he wanted to so he could leave with a clear conscience. Was the lure of the navy louder than the silent pleas of his wife?

"You left her to go do your Popeye thing, and she crashed."

He blinked. *Don't let Rico get into your head.*

They drove to Coronado and Marco made sure they stayed firmly in the flow of traffic, though he saw no signs of pursuit. Access to Coronado Island, actually a peninsula, was somewhat restricted. Visitors could cross the Coronado Bridge or take the ferry. Since it was fall, the tide of tourists had lessened, which would make it easier to spot any Pack members tailing them.

He saw no sign of trouble and neither did Dev, who showed up at the office as Marco parked the bike. "Did you explain everything to *la policia*?"

"No thanks to you," Marco said with a chuckle.

"You got plenty of hot air to do the job without me."

Dan and Angela joined them.

"Tracy is fine," Angela hastened to say, after squeezing Candace in a tight clasp. "Auntie Donna is hanging out at the Party Palace with Uncle Brent, so I could come say hello to this big lug."

Dan smiled, and Marco gave him a nod.

"Looks like you had yourselves a day," Dan said, wrapping his arm around Angela. Marco hadn't had a lot of time to get to know the doctor, but it was clear that he was head over heels for Angela, and that made him okay in Marco's book, at least for the moment.

Candace related in detail what had happened, and Angela's eyes grew wider and wider. She got up and clutched her sister's hand. "I'm starting to get really scared for you."

Candace hugged her again. "I'm okay. God's gotten me through this far, with an assist from Marco and Dev."

Baxter pushed the door open. "Officer Ridley here to see you. I figured I'd show him in."

"Thanks, Baxter," Candace said. "I think my mom will be next and—"

"And here she is," JeanBeth said, with Lon walking in right behind her. She went to Candace and hugged her tightly, kissing her on the cheek and then doing the same to Marco. She offered a solemn handshake to Dev as they made the introductions.

Lon nodded at the group and immediately went to the corner facing the door so he had sight lines for any newcomers. Old habits died hard, or not at all, Marco thought. He was positioned similarly and so was Dev. What was it like for civilians who didn't consider who might be ambushing them from behind? He figured he'd never know.

Ridley didn't waste a moment. "So? Heard from Long Beach PD that Rico almost had you. Are you ready to talk about a safe house now?"

"Already got one," Marco said.

"You were almost taken out by Rico on a public street. You need cops."

Marco bridled. "I thought we had them. Where were you? We informed you of our route and the timing. Did you even send an officer out or were we too low a priority?"

Ridley glowered. "We did send units, but they didn't get there in time. We needed more notice."

"Yeah, great protection, and by the way, I'm wondering how Rico's guys knew when we were going to show up at the courthouse in the first place," Marco snapped.

Ridley's eyes narrowed to angry slits. "They must have followed you from your safe house."

"That's not what happened."

"What are you insinuating, Quidel?"

"Just wondering, like I said."

"That's not wondering, it's accusing. You think we have a leak on our end? Not likely. Maybe it was one of your boys, here."

"It wasn't," Marco said.

JeanBeth held up a hand. "Let's keep this civil. Rico is the enemy. Marco and his men are filling the gaps because we know you have limited time and police resources. What happened today is proof of that. I don't blame you—you have a population to protect. Marco, Dev and Lon can be more focused."

Ridley spoke through his teeth. "If we had her at a safe house, we could take care of her just fine."

"I'm okay," Candace said.

"For how long?" Ridley shot a glance at Marco. "I can see I'm wasting my time here." He turned to Candace. "Call me when you realize what you're up against."

Candace's eyes flashed. "Believe me, I realize that better than anyone in this room. It's my life and my daughter's on the line here."

"Exactly why you need police protection."

She stared in silence for a moment. "Thank you. We're going to keep the status quo for now."

"All right," Ridley said. "Maybe the next attack will convince you, if you survive it." He stalked out.

"That went well," Dev said, stroking his beard. "See why I don't like talking to cops?" He put a finger to his temple. "I've got a throbbing right here."

"So what do we do now?" Dan asked. "Aside from keeping Candace and Tracy safe."

"We go on offense," Marco said.

Dan frowned. "How?"

"Put some pressure on Rico. Find a way to bring him down or at least distract him until the trial's over and Tooley is put away. Then there's no reason for Rico to continue his harassment," Marco said. "But that's going to be up to me."

"Us," Dev corrected. He got a silent nod from Lon.

"Don't you mean all of us?" Candace demanded.

"Not going to involve..." He almost said "civilians." *Don't forget that's what you are now, Marco. Not wearing that trident anymore.* Funny how being in the battle over Candace's safety kicked his navy identity to life. "I'll take care of that part. I just need information."

"No, *we'll* take care of it," Candace said. The flash in her eyes told him she was not going to back down.

"Too dangerous," he replied.

"We *are* private investigators," Candace said. "That means we don't just work on the safe cases, such as lost dogs and pilfered bingo money."

Angela nodded. "We did everything we could when Sarah was kidnapped, and all of you didn't shy away when Dan and I were in trouble in Cobalt Cove. We're in it to win it, as Dan would say."

The doctor stood and wrapped his arm around her again. "Well said. Normally I use that on the field when my softball team is playing, but it seems appropriate for this occasion, too."

Marco could see he wasn't going to win at that moment. Best to stall.

"We'll talk about it later. For now, we just need a starting point."

"Corner of Fourth and Main, in Brighton, just outside Long Beach."

They all turned to stare at Lon.

"Wow. He does talk," Dan said. "I wasn't sure."

"What's at the corner of Fourth and Main?" Candace asked.

"Chop shop. Moves around, but my guy said it's there now," Lon said. "We could do some surveillance, feed it to the cops. Put the pressure on."

And that was all Lon had to say on the subject. He resumed his slouching position and fell silent again.

Surveillance should be marginally safe if Marco could keep the Gallaghers at a reasonable distance.

“Okay,” he said. “We’ll do that part together. Who’s in?” To his pride and dismay, each and every person put a hand into the air.

TEN

Candace fumed and fretted, but there was no getting Marco to budge. She was not going to be up close to the action.

"I don't want you going along at all," Marco said. "It's not smart. You're the target, and I'm not letting you waltz up to Rico's place of business. That's just asking for disaster."

"I'm not going to get left behind minding the office," she said, louder than she should have. "This is my problem, remember? I will not cower. You may be a navy SEAL, but I'm a marine wife and we're tough as they come."

That had rendered him speechless for a few moments until he turned away grumbling, but not retreating from his position. Marco would stick to what he felt was right no matter how she railed and ranted.

She thought about Rick and how he had never backed down from a fight, either. In the present situation, he would have encouraged her, she told herself, but a niggling feeling persisted that Rick might have had similar objections to Marco's. *But you're not here, Rick, so I'm doing the best I can to be a role model for Tracy.*

The best she could do was secure a place in the car with Dan and Angela, who would park a block away, watch the video feed on their laptop and alert Marco if anyone approached. Lon and JeanBeth would be positioned in the other direction, ready to call the cops if there was any sign of trouble.

Marco drove Lon's Jeep, with Dev riding shotgun. They

took off for Brighton just after sunset at seven o'clock. Candace called Tracy on the way. She was just digging into a bowl of Neapolitan ice cream.

"So late?" Candace said. "And it's not even dessert night."

"Uncle Brent said when he's on duty I can eat all the ice cream I want." She coughed. "I have a sore throat and the cold feels good."

"Hmm. I'm going to have a talk with your uncle Brent when I get back. How bad is your sore throat?"

"Bad. When are you coming home?"

She smiled. "Why? Do you miss me or are you just trying to figure out how much ice cream you can pack away before I get back?"

Tracy went uncharacteristically silent. Candace's mother radar activated.

"Honey, what's wrong?"

Another extended pause. "I was listening to Uncle Brent talking on the phone. I know you told me not to do that, but I can't turn my ears off sometimes."

Candace knew what was coming. "I see. So you overheard him?"

"Uh-huh. He didn't know I was listening. He said there was shooting."

"It's okay. No one was hurt. We were very careful."

"But...but Daddy was careful—you said so. And he got shot, didn't he?"

Pain rippled through Candace to her core. "Yes, Daddy was careful, but that was different. He was in a war."

"There's people shooting. How's it different?"

How indeed? She felt desperate to ease Tracy's fears. "Listen, baby, Mommy is fine. Uncle Marco and his friend kept me safe. Not a scratch on me."

Her daughter let out a whoosh of air. "I knew it. Nothing can hurt you when Unco is around, right?"

Candace felt the words dry up in her mouth. Tracy idolized Marco. Marco, not Rick, not her own father. She'd elevated him to superhero status. How had Candace not noticed it before? She recalled Rick galloping around the yard with a squealing Tracy on his shoulders, yelling, "Charge!" He should be Tracy's hero.

She realized the silence had gone on too long. "Like I said, I'm okay. I will be home in a few hours. Remember to brush your teeth and say your prayers before you go to bed, and tell Auntie Donna if you start to feel real sick, okay?"

"Okay. I love you, Mommy."

There were no sweeter words in any language than those four.

"I love you, too," she said, her throat thick.

She disconnected, and Angela turned around in the front seat and blew her a kiss. Her sister had no doubt caught the emotion throbbing in her words. Angela was like that. It was what made her a spectacular chaplain. And now she was starting a new life with Dan. Candace felt gratefulness and a tiny pang of envy at the love that was so obvious between the two.

Lord, she prayed silently, *help me to keep Rick alive in Tracy's heart.* She resolved to do a better job when the whole mess was over. Tracy was scheduled to visit Rick's parents in San Diego for part of her Thanksgiving break. Candace made a mental note to ask Rick's mom to get out some photo albums to help bring Rick's memory to life for his daughter.

Marco's voice rumbled through their laptop speaker. "Checking the feed."

A video blinked to life on the laptop screen Angela held. Marco's face swam in front of the camera, his hair covered by a knit cap, the black of his clothes blending into the night. He wore eye protection and gloves.

Dev, who wore the camera, provided them a good shot

of the building. It was a two-story, run-down affair. Corroded metal siding covered the walls and stout bars crisscrossed the windows. The front lot was filled with piles of junk and strewn with rusted car parts.

"How come there are no lights showing?" Candace said.

"Dunno." Dan peered closer. "Looks like there's no one home."

Her pulse started to thrum a little faster. Was it a dead end…or a trap?

Be careful, guys. She wanted to pray, but Angela had it covered. She and Dan held hands and Candace laid her palm on her sister's shoulder as Angela prayed for safety for Marco and Dev.

Marco took the lead, allowing his eyes to adjust to the gloom instead of turning on a flashlight. They crept to the side of the building so they wouldn't be seen from the street and looked in a filthy window.

Marco couldn't discern much, but he caught enough to realize the lower floor was empty. Lon's source was wrong or they were too late. He squashed the frustration.

"Looks quiet," he mouthed.

"That's the way it always looks right before the chaos," Dev murmured.

True.

They tried the door and found it unlocked. Not a surprise. The place was most likely an abandoned building that the Pack took over for their mobile chop shop, so if they'd cleared out, there was no reason for security.

But Dev was right. Chaos could be waiting on the other side of the door. Marco pushed it open slowly, a millimeter at a time, to check for any kind of trip wire and to minimize squeaking from the rusty hinges, and listened. A faint rustling indicated maybe the place wasn't as deserted as it appeared.

He could tell Dev heard it, too. Dev was armed with a break-action pistol designed to shoot nonlethal rubber bullets, since they were, after all, civilians. Marco had his KA-BAR knife.

The bottom floor was a cavernous space, chilly and smelling of oil. Someone had done a bang-up job removing any evidence of illegal activity, but Marco knew the space they occupied was where the stolen cars would be disassembled and gutted for parts that could be sold on the black market.

He caught no movement, no further sound. Edging forward, he and Dev searched the space foot by foot, behind the drifts of torn paper and into the tiny adjoining bathroom, home to a stinking toilet and an overflowing trash can.

When their search of the garage area was concluded, they padded to the bottom of the stairwell. Dev flicked on a penlight, shielded by his palm. The steps were dirty, but the dust was disturbed. There had been some activity recently, many feet traipsing up and down by the looks of it.

Dev flicked off the light and Marco started up, Dev right behind. They kept to the edges of the stairs to minimize the noise, easing their weight down with each step. When they were two steps from the top, Marco signaled a stop so he could listen.

Nothing but silence and a soft sound behind the walls that he realized was probably the gnawing of rats.

Dev gave him an eye roll and Marco squelched a grin. On one of their South American missions where quiet was of the essence, Dev had woken up with a river rat sleeping peacefully on his bedroll. Only his torturous SEAL training kept Dev from a hollering fit to beat the band. Marco had never seen anyone have a completely silent freak-out. Dev had, of course, never lived it down.

At the moment Dev was poised and ready. *Rats or no rats*, his look said, *let's do this.*

Marco did a slow count to three and charged up, Dev following. They emerged crouched low, bodies tensed.

The top floor was also empty, a mess of discarded boxes, rusted springs and washers, part of a disassembled carburetor. Again, the place had been stripped of anything incriminating. It galled him to know the Pack was one step ahead of them again.

Marco would have left in disgust, except that the hair on his arms was standing up, his instincts telling him that they were not alone. Listening to that instinct deep in his gut was the reason he'd survived so many missions intact.

He signaled to Dev, who nodded, fingers tensed on his gun.

Marco made a half turn to his right, approaching an untidy pile of cardboard boxes. Edging close, he had his blade out, ready.

The attack came quickly, but not at him.

Someone launched himself from behind the pile and hurled a heavy toolbox. Marco recognized the guy with the missing tooth from the earlier ambush.

"Incoming," Marco shouted.

He ducked, and the box sailed over his head. Dev wasn't fast enough, and the missile deflected off his raised forearm and struck him a glancing blow on the temple. Marco heard him grunt as the impact knocked him over. Teetering on the edge of the stairs, he fell backward. The attacker raced down the steps, following Dev's tumbling path.

Marco bolted after them, outstretched fingers grazing the guy's T-shirt, grabbing hold and yanking. The fabric ripped away, leaving him with a handful of sweaty cotton. They'd reached the bottom of the steps and the guy pushed out the door. It slammed against the wall like a gunshot.

Everything in Marco wanted to chase down the man,

grab him around the neck and make him tell all he knew about Rico, but he would not leave Dev.

He raced back, finding him dazed, on his back, at the bottom of the steps.

"How bad?"

Dev opened an eye. "I'll live. Go after him, Chief."

Marco forced down the anger roiling in his gut and instead helped him to his feet.

Dev bent over for a moment, sucking in air and no doubt fighting the pain that was shooting through his head. Marco steadied him.

"Hey, sorry, Chief. Next time we'll get them."

Marco could only hope they'd have another shot at Rico.

ELEVEN

Candace cried out as the figure on the video feed leaped from behind the debris pile, tossing something. It must have struck Dev, because they heard his grunt of pain just before the camera went black.

Angela and Dan were electrified, as well.

"Stay here," Dan said, jumping from the car.

"Dan..." Angela called, but he was already sprinting down the block toward the warehouse.

Candace had to remind herself to breathe. "Don't let anyone else get hurt," she said, not realizing she'd uttered it aloud until Angela shot her a look.

Candace kept her eyes trained into the darkness while her sister radioed their mother and Lon.

"We're circling the block, trying to see which way the guy headed," JeanBeth said. "Have you heard from Marco or Dev?"

"No," Angela said. "No video feed, either. We're—"

"Look," Candace yelled, pointing into the darkness at someone running along the sidewalk. "It's the guy who took out Dev. I recognize him now. He's Rico's driver."

Angela immediately relayed the information to Lon.

"Stay put," he said. "We're coming to you."

The man was running at top speed. Candace was in agony. Once he reached the main road he would dash off into a side alley, and they'd never find him. He was close enough now for her to make out his ripped T-shirt. He would pass them in a matter of moments.

"He doesn't know we're in the car," Candace whispered.

"That's the way it's supposed to be," Angela whispered back.

"We can catch him." The man was yards away and closing fast.

"Absolutely not, Candace," Angela said.

Her sister was right—smart and practical, like always.

But this wasn't the time for practical. When he drew alongside them, Candace flung the car door open, listening with satisfaction as he ran right into it, the air whooshing out of him. Candace grabbed a can from her bag and sprang onto the sidewalk, hands clasped.

"If you move, I'll Taser you."

The guy clutched his middle, sucking in air.

Lon screeched up, slamming to a stop and leaping from the car with a bat in his hands. He looked from Candace to the guy on the ground, whose face was a mask of disgust. Lon looked in puzzlement at her hands.

"Hair spray," Candace said sheepishly. "It's pretty handy stuff when you don't have a Taser or pepper spray in your purse. It was sure awesome to have at the courthouse."

Lon smiled and stepped close, making sure the guy on the ground wasn't going anywhere.

Angela and JeanBeth examined him.

"You work for the Pack," JeanBeth said. "I've seen your pictures. Your name is Leonard, but they call you Champ."

No answer.

"You went to prison for assault," Angela said. "What are you doing here? Why did you throw the toolbox? Rico sent you, didn't he?"

Champ blinked. "I was minding my own business. Your guys blew in and scared me. I defended myself. I wasn't the one breaking and entering."

"Big picture here, Champ," JeanBeth said. "You're in

an abandoned house, all alone at night. Unless your name is on the deed, that is breaking and entering, and the cops already want to get their hands on you for the freeway ambush. You were here cleaning up evidence of the chop shop, weren't you?"

He glared angrily at her. "I'm not talking to you."

"Talk to us or the cops," Candace said, "your choice."

He stared in steely silence.

Realizing they would get no more out of Champ that way, Candace thought for a minute. "All I want to know is doesn't it make you mad that Rico plays favorites? I mean, he let you go to prison, didn't he? And here he's knocking himself out trying to free Kevin Tooley. Why?"

Champ's mouth twitched. "You're not the cops. I'm not saying a word."

Candace pressed on. "It's not an importance thing, is it? Both you and Kevin are pretty low on the totem pole, so why does Kevin get such special treatment?"

Champ growled an expletive at her until Lon tapped him with the bat.

"Don't talk to ladies like that," Lon said.

She'd clearly hit a nerve. A weakness in Rico's organization?

In the distance, Candace saw Dan, Marco and Dev walking toward them. Dev was moving gingerly, but under his own steam. She was going to call out to them, but a rumbling sound announced two vehicles approaching. Rico's people, she had no doubt.

"In the car," Lon said.

Champ jerked to his feet and took off running toward the approaching cars.

"He's getting away," she cried.

"We'll call the police," Angela said. They got back into the car, and Lon and JeanBeth did the same in theirs. Angela drove at breakneck speed to the curb, where the three men squeezed into the backseat, Candace sat in the front and quickly made the call to the police. They were off, rounding the corner just as other vehicles pulled onto the road.

Candace was nearly overwhelmed with relief that Marco appeared unhurt, but Dev had a trail of blood snaking down his temple, disappearing into his beard. Dan handed him a wad of cotton.

"Are you hurt badly, Dev?" she said.

"Nah. Just took a toolbox to the head and fell down the stairs. I've been through worse."

"He may have a concussion, but nothing's broken as best as I can tell," Dan said.

Dev looked skeptical. "No offense, but aren't you a heart doc?"

Dan chuckled. "Don't worry. They make us learn about all the parts in medical school. I know a thing or two about heads, even really hard, stubborn ones like yours."

"Good to know," Dev said, with a wan smile.

Marco frowned at Dev. "What happened? Didn't you hear me shout 'incoming'? You're supposed to duck, remember?"

Dev grinned. "Must have been too distracted by the rats."

Marco sighed and rubbed a hand over his jaw. "I'll feed the video to the cops, but basically we got nothing."

Candace thought about Champ's expression when she'd brought up the question about Kevin Tooley's treatment. "Not nothing. I'm not the only one who's wondering why Rico is so bent on protecting Kevin Tooley. Champ has been wondering, too, I can tell."

"Got ideas on how to proceed?"

She considered. "Dan, we know Kevin's mother, Yolanda, was killed in a hit-and-run while she lived in

LA. I can get the date for you. Is there any way you could track down some info about her?"

He nodded. "I might be able to rustle something up if we can dig up what hospital treated her."

"I'll find out," Angela said. "Dan and I will work that angle."

"I will, too," Candace stated. "And I think we should try and track down Champ, find out his last known address, if we can. If he's disgruntled about favoritism, maybe we can get him to give up some information on other Pack chop shops before we hand him to the cops."

They fell into silence as they drove back to Coronado. It wasn't until Marco and Candace were rolling back to the safe house in a borrowed car, with Dev in the backseat, that they brought up the subject that she knew was bothering them both.

"They knew we were coming, didn't they?" she said.

Marco nodded. "Yeah."

"Just like they knew we were going to the courthouse. How? How did the Pack get word we were coming, in time to clean up the chop shop?"

"That," Marco said his face grim, "is the million dollar question."

Marco brooded well into the night, sitting in a chair in the darkened living room when he'd finished endless laps of pacing. Dr. Dan had pushed hard for Dev to go to the hospital for a concussion check, but his patient had cheerfully declined, as Marco figured he would. As a general rule, Dev didn't like chatting with doctors any more than cops. He'd made an exception for Dan, but doctors were the people who could get a fellow scratched from a mission, and above all things, Dev couldn't tolerate that thought.

He was snoring softly in their shared room, which left Marco free to let his thoughts roll over the events of the day. Again, Rico had known they were coming, and they'd come up empty one more time. The weeks before the trial were winding down. The clock was ticking and each day increased the risk of exposure. It would take only one careless move, one small error, for Rico to find out about the safe house.

Tension roiled in Marco's gut. More pacing did not help, nor did four sets of push-ups. He picked up the tattered Bible that had accompanied him on every mission since his mother had given it to him before his first day of boot camp. He fingered the well-worn pages framed with scrawled notes he'd written in the margins.

"For God hath not given us the spirit of fear, but of power, and of love, and of a sound mind. 2 Timothy 1:7." He'd always known that fear did not come from God, which was why he didn't allow it to enter his thinking. But lately there had been tingles of uncertainty, like the cold breeze that blew in before a storm. What if he failed this time? The stakes were so unimaginably high. Tracy, Candace, the well-being of the little family that depended on him… Rick, a fellow soldier who had made the ultimate sacrifice, would expect his comrade in arms to watch over his family now that Bruce Gallagher was gone. Wouldn't he? Yes, to watch over them, but not anything more, Marco's gut told him. Candace had made that painfully clear.

He refocused on the words. *"For God hath not given us the spirit of fear; but of power, and of love..."* He repeated it silently to himself and his path became clearer, the beat of his thoughts more steady and sure. Marco would arm himself with that power and keep the love part restricted to the fond connection he'd always had with Candace. A friend to support and protect. A good friend, irreplaceable.

He sprawled on the overstuffed chair and rested the

Bible on his chest, closing his eyes as the first flutters of fatigue crept in.

Quiet footsteps roused him.

Tracy stood next to the chair, shivering in her flowered pajamas, a limp tissue in her hand and Bear at her side.

"Hey, half pint." He checked his watch. "It's almost midnight. Way past your bedtime. What are you doing up?"

"I got a cold," she said, coughing. "And I heard noises," she added, so softly he almost didn't hear.

"There's a storm coming," he said, getting up and grabbing a blanket, wrapping it around her. "The wind is blowing pretty hard."

"It's scary. Bear doesn't like it, either."

"Well, Bear's a chicken about thunder. He may need to hide under the bed if we get any."

At the sound of his name, Bear shook his head, sending his ears flapping.

Tracy didn't smile. "I don't like it, either."

"It's just noise, like you and your friends at that pool party last summer. Remember that? Man, was that loud."

She grinned. "The noise hurt your ears."

"I almost cried. Bear, too."

She was laughing now and he was gratified to hear it. "You gave me Blue Bunny that year, remember?"

"Of course I do." When she was three they'd found an orphaned rabbit underneath JeanBeth's porch. Using a baby bottle, they'd nursed the newborn along, but it had not survived more than a week. He'd been helpless to explain death to her, but Candace managed to guide Tracy through it, like she always did. To soothe the anguished child, he'd carved her a tiny bunny out of wood and painted it with her favorite colors, and it sparked a tradition. Now, back home on his boat, he was working on her bunny for this year, pink with green eyes and tiny whiskers.

Her voice was hoarse and her eyes looked puffy.

"Sore throat?"

She nodded.

He tried to think of what Candace would offer. "Want me to make you some warm milk?"

She wrinkled her nose. "Ick. Can I have hot cocoa instead?"

"Afraid not. Your mom said you've been having too much ice cream, so she's put us on sugar lockdown. Anyone who gives you a dessert has to go to the brig." He felt sure Candace would approve of that mandate. "How about some tea?"

"Okay." Tracy climbed up on the couch and Bear curled up next to her. Marco made sure the blanket was snuggled around her and her feet tucked in properly. He went to the kitchen and heated up some water, rooting around in the cupboard until he found a bag of chamomile. He dunked the bag in and waited.

As the tea steeped he considered what to say to ease her fears, weighing whether or not to give voice to his thoughts. *You're not her father*, an inner voice whispered. But there was never a bad time to talk about God, was there? "You know, half pint," he finally called softly, "you don't need to be afraid. I was just reading about that in the Bible." He quoted the verse for her. "I mean, if God says that's true, then you know it is. He's the Big Boss, and He can drive out darkness. That's something, isn't it?"

He carried the cup out to her and found she was sound asleep, Bear lying across her legs, looking at him. The lamplight shone on her delicate features, so like her mother's—and Rick's, he imagined, though he had met the man only a few times, when their time off had coincided. Tracy was so small, with thoughts that were a constant source of amazement and wonder to him. That God would put such spirit and joy in one little girl awed and humbled him. He felt honored to be a part of her world.

As he watched Tracy's peaceful breathing, he couldn't deny that he loved her, deeply and truly. Maybe it was wrong to love another man's child, but there it was, and pretending didn't make it go away. Though he couldn't ever be a father to Tracy, there was no question that he would give his life for hers in a heartbeat.

"I'll keep you safe, half pint," he whispered.

Then he gently picked her up and took her back upstairs to bed, Bear trotting dutifully behind.

TWELVE

Candace awoke to the sound of pounding rain. She wanted nothing more than to snuggle back down under the covers and close her eyes again, but hiding in bed was not an option for mothers. She'd checked on Tracy when she'd arrived back at the safe house, and thought her forehead felt warm. Several times in the night she'd heard Tracy coughing, tossing and turning.

She ran through the options in her mind. Their beloved pediatrician was back in Coronado, and she knew it would not be wise to make the trip with Tracy in the present circumstances. The prickle of worry drove her from under the covers. Donna and Tracy were not early risers, but Brent, Marco and possibly Dev would have been up at the first blush of dawn, she suspected. To prevent Uncle Brent from sneaking more sugary cereal, or worse, breakfast ice cream to Tracy, Candace slogged into a hot shower, then slipped on jeans and a long-sleeved T-shirt. She found that Tracy was not yet awake.

"Bear would be happy sleeping until noon, so he's got the perfect roomie," Marco said, as she made it downstairs.

The men were seated around the table. Brent and Dev were drinking coffee, and Marco some green concoction that looked like something scooped from the surface of a pond.

"Kale smoothie. Want me to fix you one?"

She politely declined and helped herself to tea and toast. "How are you doing, Dev?"

He fingered the small bandage taped to his eyebrow. "Toolbox one, Dev zero," he said with a grimace.

"We're looking for an address for Champ, though he's probably on the move now that the police are onto him." Marco drummed his fingers on the tabletop. "When we find him, I'm going to pay him a visit and see if he will give us anything on Rico."

Dev frowned. "Don't see how that's gonna work. He's Pack, Rico's driver no less. He's not gonna turn on the lead dog."

"But he's been to prison," Candace said, "and Rico did nothing to bail him out."

Brent stretched out his tall, lanky frame. "Donna and I burned the midnight oil and we found out that Champ's brother Martin was Pack, too, but he messed up some deals, talked too much to the cops and he was beaten up pretty bad. Left California and hasn't been heard from since."

Candace sat up straighter. "So Champ's got more reasons to be angry at Rico."

Marco nodded. "All we need is one break, a location where we can find a working chop shop. Find it, call the cops and they might have enough to arrest Rico. Champ can give us that once we find him. In any case, it will cause Rico a whole batch of problems to focus on besides Candace's testimony against Kevin Tooley."

A cough from upstairs intruded on Candace's growing enthusiasm. She hastened to Tracy, who swiped at her runny nose with a tissue, while Bear licked a spot on her wrist.

"Don't feel good, baby?"

"No. Throat hurts." Tracy closed her eyes again. "Don't wanna get up."

Decision time. Wait it out or go find a doctor? Tracy was susceptible to strep, which she'd had once already during the school year. Best to call Dan. It was a great thing to have a doctor added to the family. Now, if they could just recruit a dentist, and possibly a plumber, into the Gallagher clan she'd be all set.

She jogged back downstairs and Skyped Angela at the office to ask where she might find Dan.

"He's sitting right here next to me and he's got some info for you."

Dan appeared, slouching to get his face in the screen. "Got a lead for you on Kevin Tooley's mom."

The others stopped talking in order to listen in.

"It turns out that the doctor who treated Yolanda is a colleague of mine. His name is Wesley Finch. We met at a few trainings over the years. Good guy, lousy golfer. He actually does some volunteer hours at a Long Beach clinic about a half hour from your current location. He should be in today if you want to give him a call. I told him you might be contacting him."

Again, the uprising of hope. Candace knew the others might not agree with the rabbit trail she was following, but something kept urging her in that direction. "Dan, you're the best."

Angela smiled. "Isn't he, though?"

Brent rolled his eyes, but Candace enjoyed the obvious adoration that flowed between the pair. She asked Dan about Tracy's symptoms.

"Is she running a temp?"

"I don't know. I didn't bring a thermometer, but she feels warm to me."

"If you think it's safe, take her to Dr. Finch's clinic for a throat culture. It's on Stowe Street. I'll call and let him know you're coming."

"No, Doc," Marco said. "The less people who know our plans the better. You sure you can't come here and treat her?"

"Pediatrics isn't my field, but I would if I wasn't on my way to the hospital to prep for surgery. It's going to be a long procedure and I'd feel more comfortable if Tracy had that swab sooner rather than later."

"All right," Marco said. "We'll make that happen today. Hope that surgery goes well."

"It will," Dan said. "I'm the best cardiac surgeon in the world, Angela tells me."

She laughed. "He's awesome with a needle and thread. He mended a loose hem for me this morning."

Dan wriggled his fingers. "Hearts, hems. I'm thinking of taking up knitting next."

"Real manly, Doc," Brent said.

"This from a guy who sews his own Coast Guard gear."

"Don't think I'd trust it to anyone else, do you?" Brent said.

Candace laughed as they signed off. She marveled at how Brent and Dan had enriched the lives of the Gallagher women. Brent with his goofy sense of humor, and Dan, brilliant and alternately self-deprecating and cocky. And Marco, though he was not her partner, brought his own steady faith, dry wit and tough-guy persona to the clan.

But there should be another at the family table. Rick should be there with his arm around Candace, participating in the good-natured ribbing and tending to his sick little girl. Instead there was a vacant chair, an empty spot in her heart and Tracy's. A dull ache throbbed inside her, but it was not the same kind of pain that had accompanied her after his death and the loss of their baby. That was an excruciating, fiery anguish that seared through her every nerve. Now, almost six years after his death, the pain had morphed into a hollow, cold discomfort, which scared her deep down. Was Rick slipping into distant memory as the days and years ticked by?

Was Candace forgetting her husband and soul mate? She

found her jaw was clenched, and she breathed out slowly. No, she would not let it happen.

I'll always keep that spot at the table for you, Rick, she thought as she got up. *I'll never let anyone else fill it.* She left the men to their planning and took her mug and plate to the sink to wash them.

She felt Marco's presence as she put the dishware away, but didn't look at him.

"You okay?" he asked, after a momentary hesitation.

"Sure."

"You looked kind of… I don't know. Pensive."

She turned to face him then. "Marco, did you ever…" She trailed off. She should not be asking Marco, not about this.

"It's okay. You can ask, whatever it is."

She tried to funnel her cascade of feelings into one essential question. "After the divorce—after Gwen, um, moved on to other relationships—did you ever worry that she would forget you?"

His eyes crinkled at the edges, and she wondered why she had asked. It was an unhealed cut, and she'd probed it with the question.

"Actually, I guess I worried more that she wouldn't."

"What do you mean?"

His long silence made her think he might have changed his mind about answering, but then he rested his hands on his waist and exhaled. "I wished Gwen would forget all the times I let her down."

"She was a drug addict, Marco. She let *you* down."

He seemed lost in thought as he stared out the kitchen window into the falling rain. "Gwen's mom died when she was a teen. Her dad raised her, worked two jobs and never really had time for her. Gwen was shy, desperate for him to love her, but he just couldn't, not the in the way she needed, and she didn't know how to ask him." Marco's mouth twisted. "I don't think she knew how to ask me, either. She took what I gave her, but it wasn't enough."

Candace listened, unwilling to interrupt. It was more than he had ever said about Gwen.

"I've been thinking a lot about it lately, and it would be easy to say she was a drug addict and she ruined our marriage and her life. But the fact is I was selfish. I joined the navy right out of high school because I wanted to, and Gwen went along with it. I knew she was unhappy, lonely in our military housing. She never was the type to make friends easily. She wanted to fit in, but she didn't click with the other wives. They were polite and everything, but she didn't fit into their social circles and it left her lonely. I knew all that, but I signed up for SEAL training, anyway. I told myself she'd be all right, that the rehab time would stick and all my love and support had been enough to strengthen her. I think I knew, deep down, that she might not be able to stay clean, but what I wanted, to be a navy SEAL, was more important than what she needed."

The sadness in his voice cut Candace to the core. "Marco, you're too hard on yourself."

His eyes shone with repressed grief. "Just telling the truth."

"Service isn't selfishness. You made the best choice you could at the time."

A small smile, mournful and so humble it broke her heart, crimped his mouth.

"Candace, I was busy being the hero of my own life when she needed me to be the hero in hers."

She reached out and placed a hand on his chest, feeling the steady beat there underneath the wall of muscle. She wanted to take the hurt, to draw it out of him and set him free from the poison. "You can't—"

He took her hand gently, held it to his lips and kissed her wrist. "Yeah," he whispered. "I can, because that's what happened. I've asked God for forgiveness and I believe He has granted it to me, but the problem is..."

His eyes locked on hers.

"I never asked Gwen to forgive me." He shook his head. "I never asked her and now she's gone."

Candace held his hand and they listened to the rain coursing off the roof and down the walls. The irony was inescapable. They were two people grappling with the past. She didn't want to let go of her lost love, and Marco was chained to what he saw as his own betrayal of Gwen.

"What a mess we make of things, don't we?" she whispered.

He nodded. "Guess that's why we need a Savior."

A sweet thought circled in her heart. What would it be like if she and Marco could let go of the pain together? God offered hope and a future, didn't He? The freedom from fear and the balm of forgiveness? The idea thrilled her. But stepping forward with Marco would mean turning her back on Rick and on her vows to love and be faithful to him forever.

Marco and Rick. Two good men, but to one she'd given a forever promise not just for herself, but for her daughter.

She let go of his hand. "Tell me how we're going to get my baby to the doctor."

Marco and Dev mapped out the route to the clinic. It would be better if Donna took Tracy, and Candace stayed in the safe house, but Marco didn't waste any breath suggesting that one. He'd done quite enough talking for one morning. Too much sharing with a woman who seemed to draw the truth out of him like honey from a hive. How she did it he did not know, but he resolved to keep his mouth shut and his eyes open. *Try a dose of self-control, why don't you?*

The route was simple, very public, and the clinic itself

was a squat three-story building set in the middle block of a quiet street.

Brent and Donna drove them in Donna's van.

Dev leaned down into the open driver's window. "Driving a minivan, Coastie? This is bad for your macho reputation."

Brent feigned irritation. "I'll have you know my wife is a veterinarian, and this van has transported everything including a litter of pigs."

Dev raised an eyebrow. "That doesn't up the cool factor."

"Some of us don't need motorcycles to be cool."

Dev headed for his bike, laughing as he went.

Marco rode shotgun and Tracy, Donna and Candace squeezed in the back. Tracy was still in her pajamas, bundled in a blanket, with duck slippers on her feet.

"Ready?" Marco asked.

"Ready," Tracy croaked. "But do I hafta go to the doctor?"

"Yes," Marco, Candace, Donna and Brent all said at once.

"Can I have ice cream after?"

"No," the same four voices replied.

"But I'll play you a game of checkers when you're feeling better," Brent said. "And I'm going to win this time."

It's about time we get a win for this family, Marco thought, as he checked one more time out the side-view mirrors before Brent pulled out onto the road.

THIRTEEN

Dev took off first to scout and check out the clinic. Brent took it slow to give him a head start. Since Dev had a lead foot on the gas, Marco figured their leisurely pace would be adequate. For his part, he saw no signs of anything unusual.

Candace asked at the front desk if Dr. Finch was available and the nurse slotted them into a third-floor room to wait. Marco leaned against a wall inside the exam room while Candace helped Tracy up onto the paper-covered table. Nurses, orderlies and an occasional patient roamed the hallways.

Dr. Finch was a short, stocky man who greeted Marco with a firm handshake. "Tracy's father?"

"Honorary uncle."

Dr. Finch chatted with Candace and Tracy, and did a throat culture, which made Tracy gag. Marco gave her a thumbs-up when she'd managed to make it through.

Her rueful smile amused him. He'd seen the same look on her mother's face more times than he could count.

"I'll call you in the next twelve hours with the results." Dr. Finch looked at his chart. "What is your cell phone number?"

"You can call Dan," Marco interjected. "He'll relay the message."

Dr. Finch's brow crimped ever so slightly, but he nodded. "Okay. Not the usual, but I have the utmost respect for Dan. He tells me you had a question about a former patient of mine. Shall we step outside and chat about that?"

Candace kissed Tracy, who was engrossed in the animal magazine the nurse had given her to peruse. "Be right back."

In the hallway, Candace thanked him for chatting with them about Yolanda Tooley. "As I explained, I'm testifying in her son's murder trial and we're trying to piece together some facts about his mother's life."

Dr. Finch balled his hands in his pockets and jingled whatever metallic things he had in there before cocking his head. "It took me a while to decide whether or not I should talk to you. Patient privacy is something I don't take lightly, but since Yolanda Tooley is deceased, I believe it is okay to discuss some generalities of the case with you."

"Thank you," Marco said.

Candace nodded her thanks, as well. "I'd welcome any information you can give me about her."

He looked up at the ceiling for a moment. "If my memory serves, she was found in the street, the victim of a hit-and-run. I treated her in the emergency room for extensive internal bleeding, as well as a spinal fracture and a brain hemorrhage. As you know, she did not survive."

Dr. Finch's mouth pinched. Marco felt a kinship with the man in that moment. His was the look of someone who had done all he could, exercised every bit of training and skill he possessed, and lost anyway. Angela had told him that Dr. Dan kept a notebook with names of those he had not been able to save. Marco had one also, locked away deep down inside his mind, a comprehensive list of the brothers he'd lost in battle. Gwen was written in tears there, as well. He suspected Dr. Finch had his own list, too.

Candace was looking at Dr. Finch with that tiny quirk of the head that meant she'd detected a curious nuance that had eluded Marco.

"You look as though there was something about the case

that was not so cut-and-dried," she said. "It might help us to hear your thoughts."

Finch stared as if he was looking somewhere inside his memory. "My case report is clear and comprehensive. The police never caught the driver as far as I know. I believe her son was sent to live with a relative, an uncle or aunt. Her mother was contacted, but she was too ill to make the trip to the hospital, as I recall."

"So what bothers you about the case?"

His mouth quirked. "I'm not sure I should say. Conjecture sometimes makes things worse."

"Please," Candace said, her brown eyes so soft with entreaty that Marco would have told her anything. "It's very important."

"There was both old and new bruising around the throat."

"Old?" Marco said. "Indicating a pattern of abuse?"

He huffed out a breath. "Possibly. It wasn't what killed her ultimately, but I did tell the police."

"So you suspect the hit-and-run driver was the same person who hurt her previously?" Candace said.

"I can't say for sure, but the car that hit her did not slow down," Finch said. "There were no brake marks and nothing to indicate he or she stopped and considered helping her before fleeing the scene. To me, that hints at some impairment or…"

"Or what?" Marco pressed.

"Hatred."

Yes, it would take a heart full of hatred to intentionally run a woman down in the street, Marco thought.

Finch looked from him to Candace. "I have nothing, no proof, just the instincts of an old doctor who has seen too much of man's inhumanity to man in his time in the emergency room."

"Instincts are everything, Doc," Marco said.

"Not enough to change much in this case." He pulled

a vibrating cell phone from his pocket and checked the screen. "I'm needed downstairs. I'll call Dan when the culture comes back."

They said goodbye and watched him go.

Marco gave Candace a minute before he asked, "Tell me where you're going with this."

"I'm not sure."

"Even if the death of Kevin Tooley's mother was murder, not an accident, how does that help us?"

Candace appeared lost in thought. "Just a feeling," she finally said, "but someone I know said instincts are everything."

He chuckled. "Someone probably doesn't know what he's talking about."

She pushed a lock of hair behind her ear. "Well, someone has done pretty well so far, so I'm going to think about what my instincts are trying to tell me."

"Fair enough. Time to… I mean, is it okay to pack up Tracy and get moving?"

"Yes," she said. "And thanks for making it a question, not a command. Be right back."

A question, not a command. *Maybe you're learning after all, Marco.*

She returned to the exam room and he checked his phone. Dev was circling the building on the ground floor. All quiet except the usual clinic business.

The elevator doors opened and Brent stepped out, holding a ducky slipper. "Found this in the car. Didn't want her right foot to catch a chill."

"She's—" Marco didn't finish the sentence as the stairwell door opened and Champ poked his head in. His eyes flashed in recognition, but not surprise. This wasn't a coincidental meeting at the clinic.

Marco sprinted toward him, shouting to Brent over his shoulder, "Get the girls out!"

He slammed through the door, in time to hear Champ's shoes squeaking as he took the stairs two at a time. Marco radioed Dev. Then he vaulted over the railing dropping straight down to the second-floor landing, cutting the distance between himself and his quarry.

The exam room door shot open as Candace was searching for Tracy's other slipper.

"They're here. Gotta go," Brent said. "Marco's chasing down Champ."

Fear thundered through her. Not again. Not with her daughter in the line of fire.

Brent scooped up Tracy, then peeked out the door and listened. "I'm going to make a run for the elevator. If there's anyone bad in it, we'll retreat into the nearest exam room and barricade the door, okay?"

She managed a nod. Keeping as close as she could, she scurried along behind him.

They didn't get far. The elevator doors opened. Inside stood Shoe Guy, who had tried to kill Candace in the college parking lot. With an evil smile, he reached behind him. Brent gripped Tracy tighter as they backed away. There was no way they would be able to get to the exam room.

"The stairs," Candace screamed.

Brent was already sprinting in that direction, shouting at her to follow. "We've got an intruder," he hollered to a nurse, who ran immediately for the phone.

Candace whirled to follow Brent just as a shot exploded the cabinet door behind her, sending shards of glass tumbling through the air. She dropped down behind a laundry cart. An orderly took cover in a doorway near her, his eyes wide with fright.

The elevator doors closed. Her breathing sounded so loud in her own ears she wasn't sure she could detect signs that Shoe Guy was still there or not. He might have retreated to another floor. She saw a nurse and a doctor scurrying to shut patient doors, and talking into radios, following their safety protocols.

Had Brent made it to the stairs with Tracy? It was the only thing that mattered. If she kept her pursuer close, he couldn't go after them. The delay might allow them to get clear of the building.

Hurry, Brent, she willed. *Get her out of here.*

Creeping a few feet forward, she tried to take a look. At first she saw nothing, but she heard the tiniest scuff of a shoe on the tile floor. She froze as the sound drew closer to her hiding place. A patient peeked out of a room, mouth open in shock. Candace gestured for her to retreat and phone for help.

Crouched behind the laundry, she heard footsteps. Her fingers turned to ice as she clutched the end of the cart. It was too late to run and too soon to expect help from security. She readied herself behind the cart, trying to quiet her gasping breaths. Only a few feet separated Candace from the man who she knew had been ordered to kill her. Sucking in a shaky breath, she tensed. When she saw the top of his head appear, she shoved the laundry cart with all her strength.

It caught him in the stomach and he went over onto his back with a grunt, arms and legs splayed out. She didn't hesitate, but sprinted to the second elevator, smacking the buttons with panicked fingers.

The ding was the most comforting sound she'd ever heard. The doors slid open, and this time the elevator was empty. Behind her, the orderly took off, running after the fleeing Shoe Guy. She jabbed the button repeatedly and the metal walls began to close around her. Before the doors could seal her off completely, Jay Rico appeared in the gap, reached out his hands and wrapped them around her throat. Futilely, she clawed at them as he dragged her from the elevator.

"Hey, baby. What's your hurry?" he whispered in her ear. She tried to scream, but the pressure on her windpipe prevented it. Feet slipping against the tile, her hands trying to pry loose his arm, she was forced back into the room where Dr. Finch had examined Tracy.

Rico said in her ear, "Stop struggling. My boys have your daughter. If you give me trouble, I'll have them kill her. Got me?"

Candace went limp, her lungs unable to draw sufficient breath.

He increased the pressure until she thought her throat would collapse. "I said, do you understand me?"

She managed a nod. He released his grip, and she scooted away from him, scuttling back against the wall, gasping. He wore a black jacket and jeans, his shirt scrolled with some sort of fancy print she couldn't decipher. His hair was loose, black waves that melded with the shadows of his clothing, a scruff of beard darkening his jaw.

Maybe he was bluffing about having Tracy. It would be just his style, to terrorize her with the thing she feared the most. Her only option was to buy time until Dev and Marco could find Brent and then get Tracy to safety. They had to. She couldn't think about any other possibilities or she would become too paralyzed to keep herself alive. "Don't hurt my daughter."

He shook his head in disgust. "Still giving orders? You brought this on her." He jabbed a finger in her direction. "You. All you had to do was refuse to testify, and you and your kid could have walked away safely. But you didn't." His expression was incredulous. "And now you think you should dictate terms?"

"I'm testifying against Tooley because I want my daughter to know what's right."

"What's right," he said, "is taking care of your family. But here you are, going to get yourself killed, and then it's game over and there's nothing changed for all your heroism."

"There's a life after this one," she said with a gulp. "Don't you believe that?"

He rolled his eyes. "We gonna start up with that religion stuff? My grandma used to tell me, 'Jay boy, you need some humility. Greatest are gonna become the least in the end.' Well, I'm only interested in the first part." His eyes shone. "In my world, I am the greatest. I control a whole network, a half-dozen chop shops, and I got more money and power than I know what to do with. Everyone thinks about me. Some people adore me, others are scared of me and some just plain hate me, but everybody knows my name. I made my choice, you see?"

"You have a chance to change. It's not too late. Your grandma was right. She was trying to show you that God—"

He laughed. "Don't go all Bible on me, baby. I ain't leaving this world until I take every last thing that I want and finish my business. If God's gonna judge me for my sins after I die, then there'll be plenty of other folks in that line." His jaw tensed as he stared at her. "Folks who wronged me and my kin."

"What about the people you wronged?"

"They crossed me, they earned it."

"Some of them didn't. You've hurt people who didn't deserve it, haven't you? Innocent people."

Something flickered in the depths of his eyes. "No more time for this. You so sure about where you're going when you die, then might as well get started." He grabbed her wrist and shoved her through the fire escape door onto the metal platform outside. She resisted, but he was strong and he twisted her arms behind her. The spatter of drizzle hit her face, slithering down her neck. Rico didn't seem to notice as the droplets spangled his hair.

"Climb up on the railing."

She couldn't believe what he was telling her. "What?"

He leaned so close his mouth touched her ear. "I said climb up on the railing."

She still didn't fully understand, so he cinched her arms so tightly she cried out from the pain.

"So you can jump," he hissed in her ear.

Her throat closed in terror. "No," she gasped.

"Headfirst, three stories, probably gonna kill you but maybe not. Maybe just paralyze you or bust up your legs and arms." He chuckled. "It's okay, though. You know where you're going and all."

Horror rippled through her. "I am not going to jump."

His hair grazed her cheek as he pushed her against the railing. She could smell his cologne, cloying, dizzying, filling up the air around her. "Yes, you are. It's neater than me shooting you. No bullets to trace."

"No," she whispered.

"You see what I'm doing for you here, don't you? Your kid will live, and she will know you did the right thing. That's what you wanted, huh? That's why you're so bull-headed about testifying? I'm letting you do the right thing to save your daughter. I am helping you do exactly what you want without the need for a trial. You should be thanking me."

She shook her head. It couldn't be happening like this. *God, help me.*

Her fingers clung to the railing, metal biting into her skin.

He let go of her arms and stepped back. "Not got a lot of time here, baby, and my people can't keep hospital security busy forever. Climb up on the edge and jump," Rico rasped. "Or I will tell my guy to kill your girl."

What choice did she have? None at all. Her only hope was that Marco or the police would see her there, perched on the railing, and capture Rico before she plunged to the street below. Body trembling, Candace grasped the metal stairs above for support and pulled one knee up on the narrow railing.

"That's it," Rico said with a nod of encouragement. "You got this."

When she thought her limbs wouldn't obey, he palmed his cell phone and dialed. "Yeah, D.J. Got her? Good." He covered the phone. "Gonna tell him to take her to the beach. Somewhere lonely where no one will hear her scream."

"No," Candace sobbed. She hoisted herself up onto the railing and teetered there, arms stretched above her, clutching the stairs that led up to the roof for support.

"Okay, then." Rico gave her a nod of encouragement, as if he was some sort of psychotic coach. "All you gotta do is let go of the stairs there and jump. If I were you I'd try to go headfirst. Might as well make it clean."

It was as if her body and her mind were disconnected. The only part that seemed to work was her heart, throbbing a silent plea to God. If she didn't jump, Tracy would die. If she did, she would be throwing away all the precious moments that lay ahead for her and her daughter, leaving Tracy with a legacy of loss.

Rock and a hard place. Candace had never really grasped the significance of that phrase before.

Rock and a hard place.

She didn't want to die. Where was Marco? Dev? Anyone who could save her and rescue her daughter.

The wind seemed to whistle a low and mournful dirge in her ears.

Tracy, I love you.

FOURTEEN

In spite of his jump down the stairwell, Marco didn't catch up with Champ until the first floor. After a flying tackle, he turned the thug over and grabbed him by the throat.

"Came to warn you," Champ said, lips drawn taut, accentuating the gap left by his missing tooth.

"Oh, yeah. I'm sure you did." Marco hauled him to his feet and shoved out the stairwell door, a spatter of rain hitting his face.

"No, really," Champ said. "Rico's out of control. He's gonna bring us all down."

"Tell it to the cops." Marco marched him toward the front of the building.

"Listen to me. He has a plan. They're gonna—"

Dev sprinted up. "They had intel. Knew we were coming again. I…" His eyes rounded in an expression Marco had never seen before on his friend's face. His gaze was riveted to a spot somewhere above them. Marco swiveled to look.

The bottom dropped out of his stomach. Three stories up, Candace stood teetering on the narrow railing of the fire escape, one hand gripping the metal above her.

Marco let go of Champ and charged to the first-floor fire escape. He pounded up to the second floor, taking the steps three at a time, his weight vibrating the steel slats under his feet. One thought echoed with each step.

Don't let her fall. Don't let her fall. Don't—

A shot erupted from above him and scorched a trail

of heat past his shoulder. Candace screamed, still clutching the rail.

From below him, Dev let loose with some counterfire. Because the building was full of civilians, he aimed for a spot above the window and fired off some of the rubber-tipped bullets he'd loaded, to lessen the chance of injuring an innocent bystander. It was an awkward angle, Marco knew, since Rico was sheltering inside the building, but the bullets stopped his attack for a precious moment more.

Marco propelled himself up toward the third-floor landing, three steps, six. He was almost to Candace, close enough that he could see the frozen disbelief on her face. Dev had stopped firing, which told Marco he'd headed inside, intending to circle around and cut off Rico's escape. But would it be in time?

Rico squeezed off another shot, and it was so close to Candace's face that she jerked backward, losing her grip. A siren wailed in the distance.

Marco sprang, leaping the last few feet. His fingers searched for her, slipping, grazing the fabric of her jacket sleeve.

No!

Time seemed to slow down. The silver raindrops tumbled as she fell. At the last moment, his fingers found her wrist. His desperate grasp stopped her downward motion, the momentum nearly taking him over the railing, as well. He hung there, the metal cutting into his stomach, every bone and tendon strained as he held her dangling in the air by one wrist.

Her eyes found his, her face damp with rain.

I won't let you fall, he wanted to say, but he couldn't spare the breath.

Moisture made his grip even more tenuous as he braced himself against the steel bars with his legs, snagging her other wrist. Sweat popped out on his forehead, mingling with the falling rain.

For a moment he could only hang on, steeling his muscles against the ferocious pull of gravity and the assault of pain. Slowly, he began to pull her toward safety. Inch by inch he dragged her closer. He wondered if Dev had got Rico, or if there would be another shot fired from behind him at any moment. It was a variable he couldn't control. Dev would do his job, or Marco would be shot in the back and he and Candace would both die, but he was not going to let go of her. In spite of his incremental progress, his grip began to loosen as she became too weary to help hold on.

"Candace," he grunted.

She looked at him, dangling helplessly, her rain-soaked clothes making her heavier. One hand slipped loose from his grasp, and panic roared inside him.

I will not let you fall.

The metal of the fire escape groaned as he tried to better secure her. He could hold her in place for a while longer, but didn't have the leverage to pull her up by one wrist.

"You gotta help me, Candace," he grunted. "Help me, honey."

She tried feebly to raise her other arm and grab hold, but she was too depleted. Fear and defeat crept into her gaze.

I...will...not...let...you...fall.

His shoulders began to tremble with the excruciating effort. Marco breathed through the pain, drawing on reserves from way down deep.

With every nerve screaming in displeasure, he began to pull her up, inch by torturous inch.

Brent burst from the building onto the fire escape, reaching over to grab Candace's sodden jacket. Still, Marco didn't let up a fraction.

Together they hoisted her up until they were able to ease

her onto the landing. Marco collapsed next to her, unable to get his muscles to respond to any kind of orders from his brain. Their faces upturned to the rain, they gasped together, sucking in lungfuls of precious air, until he finally got himself into a sitting position.

Brent bundled Candace back inside the clinic and set her on the exam table, and Marco trailed after, sinking into a chair. He sat panting, his muscles twitching from the abuse. Her hand found his as Brent checked her over for injuries.

"Tracy," she sobbed. "He said he'd kill Tracy if I didn't jump."

Brent tried to soothe her. "It's okay. You're safe now."

She struggled to a sitting position against his restraining grasp. "Don't you understand? He's got Tracy."

"No, he doesn't," Brent said firmly.

She stared at him. "What?"

"I took Tracy out of the clinic after we got separated, and handed her to Donna."

"Rico doesn't have her?" Candace whispered.

"No. Tracy is safe. We'll get you to her as soon as you can stand. Dev said the building is clear. Rico got away again."

Candace let go of Marco's hand, turned on her side and began to sob. Brent looked at Marco.

"Give her a minute," Marco said, grateful that he, too, would have time to get his body back in line.

Brent nodded. "I'll call the others. Watch for shock."

"Yeah."

A security guard charged through the door. "We're okay," Marco said. With a nod, the man whirled away to continue his sweep of the floor.

Marco thought through the next block of time in his mind. There would be cops. Lots of them. Questions. Candace looked so small curled up on that exam table. Rico had made her think that the only way to save Tracy was to sacrifice her own life. It tore at Marco worse than any pain he could remember. Rico was not just a terrorist, he was a monster.

With agonizing effort, Marco stood and rested his hands on her head. He wanted to pray aloud, but the words wouldn't come. Instead, he stayed still, breathing with her.

He couldn't erase the terrible reality of what had just happened to her, but he could spare her from any more trauma, at least for tonight. He sucked in a breath and fought through the agony in his body.

"Gonna get you out of here. I'll stay to talk to the cops."

She didn't answer, didn't move.

He smoothed a hand over her wet hair. Still no response. "Candace, can you walk?"

She was sobbing quietly, her face shrouded by her hair. He pulled a sheet from the shelf above the bed and wrapped it around her. With a brutal effort that strained every sinew, he picked her up and walked down to the van, where he knew Brent and Tracy would be waiting.

Candace held her daughter all the way back to the safe house. Tracy was full of questions, because Brent had gotten her out of the clinic before she'd witnessed any violence. Candace was deeply grateful. She knew she should feel other things, too, like anger and relief and fear, but now she was numb, cold on the outside and frozen to the core.

Her mind couldn't process what had happened. It was as though she was watching bits and pieces from a bad movie. Brent drove, and Donna kept sneaking worried glances at her from the corner of her eye as they went, Dev trailing behind them on his motorcycle. She wanted to ask about Marco, but simply couldn't make her mouth work. Flashes of his face, his hands gripping hers, the agony in his eyes, darted through her mind.

When they arrived, Brent took Tracy off to find Bear. Angela hugged Candace, stroking her hair and whispering to her. Candace was mute. Angela pulled her to arm's length and seemed to peek inside, as if she understood the confused misfiring of Candace's heart. And maybe she did. Maybe this was what Angela's PTSD felt like, as if she was trapped in a well of black emotion. Candace took her sister's hand and squeezed. It was the only gesture she could manage.

"Come with me," Angela said. "You need a hot shower."

Do I? Candace thought dully. She didn't even know what she needed, and was grateful to let her sister take charge.

Angela led her to the bathroom and started the water, adjusting the temperature until steam began to fill the tiny space. She helped Candace off with her clothes and guided her under, sliding the shower curtain closed.

"I'll be sitting right outside the bathroom door," Angela said.

And then there was the comfort of hot water and noise that seemed to mute the memories of what had happened, at least for the fifteen minutes she was in the shower. She tried hard not to think, just to feel the warmth. When the water started to run cold, she turned off the tap and Angela was there with a towel, her pajamas and a robe.

She guided Candace to the bed.

"Auntie?" Tracy asked from the doorway, tentative. "Can I see Mommy?"

Angela looked questioningly at Candace.

Candace pulled back the covers. "I saved a spot for you," she said, her voice cracking.

Tracy hopped into the bed. A second later Bear catapulted up, too, rooting around until he found a comfortable space.

Angela started to shoo him off.

"Let them stay," Candace said. "We'll be okay."

After a moment, Angela nodded. "Call me for anything," she said.

Tracy's arms went around her mother's waist. Candace stroked the soft skin of her cheeks. "We'll get you some medicine for your sore throat soon, baby."

"Okay. Mommy, are we ever going to get to go home? I feel scared here. I miss school and my friends. I'm tired of all this sneaking around."

"We'll be home soon. Very soon." Candace sighed, feeling the ache in her wrists where Marco's grasp had kept her from falling. He'd managed this time, but how much longer could they outwit Rico?

Something deeper prickled her soul. She'd stared into his eyes when he held her and glimpsed into the deepest part of him, seeing a tide of emotion so transparent that it could not be mistaken for anything else but love. The realization washed through her like a wave, both exhilarating and terrifying. A part of her wanted to wade into that tide, to lose herself to the promise of a new love with a God-fearing man who would sacrifice everything for her.

Then the rush of guilt took its place. Rick was her husband and he would always be her husband. She could not betray him by giving her heart to another man, not even Marco Quidel.

"I was thinking about your father, baby," she said. "Do you want to hear about the time he found the kittens in our basement?"

"Okay, Mommy," Tracy said, and Candace began to bring her husband's memory alive.

They talked for a long while, then Candace must have dozed, because when she opened her eyes, Tracy and Bear had gone. There was a quiet tap on the door. Angela stuck her head in.

"Ready for reinforcements?"

"What do you mean?"

She stepped aside to admit Donna and Brent, JeanBeth, Lon and Dan, Tracy piggybacked on the doctor's shoulders.

Her mother reached her first. "I told Lon I was coming with or without him. He wisely decided to bring me." She kissed Candace, who couldn't hold back the tears. JeanBeth smoothed her hair as she'd done through all the enormous ups and downs of Candace's life—the incredible blessing of Tracy's birth, the day she'd gotten the news about Rick. Through Candace's miscarriage, the loss of Bruce, the privilege of watching Tracy in every school program, swim meet and Christmas morning for nearly eight years. Until she'd had Tracy, Candace didn't fully understand the depth of a mother's love. Now she did, and she submerged herself in it gratefully.

When her tears relented, she wiped her face. "Isn't it dangerous for you to be here?"

"Would have been dangerous for Lon not to let her come," Dev said, socking the other man in the shoulder.

Lon smiled. "Wasn't followed."

"How do you know?" Donna said. After a moment she waved a hand. "Never mind. I don't really need to know that, do I?"

"Not really, ma'am," Dev said.

Candace looked around. "Where's Marco?"

"Still with the cops. I had to talk with them, too, after I escorted you back here." He grimaced. "They were not terribly warm and welcoming, and I've got a tension headache to prove it."

Her heart sank. After the physical beating Marco had just taken, saving her, he was now enduring an interrogation from law enforcement to spare her more discomfort.

JeanBeth stood. "So it's time for some serious praying." Angela, Donna, her mother and Tracy joined hands together. The men stepped to the back of the room, and Lon and Dev headed for the door.

Donna giggled. “I think we scared ’em.”

“Oh, Lon’s just shy, I think,” JeanBeth said. “He’s been working through a Bible study with me, though.”

Candace gaped. “You’re kidding.”

“No,” she said, innocently. “It’s been a couple of decades since he’s been to church, so we’re doing some reading at home until he feels more comfortable.”

“You’re amazing, Mom,” Donna said.

JeanBeth shrugged. “It only required some gentle encouragement.”

“That’s a Gallagher for you,” Angela said.

Candace laughed, the grip of the horrifying events loosening as her family filled the room with prayer.

FIFTEEN

Marco was offered a bottle of water at the police station. He could really have used a fistful of aspirin and a couple ice packs to dull the fiery pain shooting through his ribs. He'd probably cracked a few and definitely strained every muscle in his torso, but Candace was safe, so he counted it all as a win.

He tried to refocus on Ridley and Barnes, who must have figured he didn't have any other place to go. It was the only reason he could imagine for them to be asking the same questions over and over, after the Long Beach PD had done their initial investigation.

"We need to talk to Candace," Barnes said.

"She'll call you after she's rested."

"That's not acceptable." She leaned forward, elbows on the table. "Rico made his move in public this time and no one else can ID him except her. We have witnesses to Rico's right-hand man, but she's the only direct link besides you."

"What about his second guy? Or the one from the parking lot attack? I call him Shoe Guy."

"Shoe Guy escaped, and since your backup let Champ go," Ridley said, "we've got nothing."

"My backup had bigger problems, namely helping me keep Candace from falling."

"Don't you get it?" Ridley said, smacking a hand on the tabletop. "Rico's inches from killing her because you and your massive ego are refusing to allow us to help."

Lid on the temper, Marco. "This isn't ego."

"Oh, that's exactly what this is. You think you're smarter,

stronger and better trained than law enforcement, don't you?"

Barnes cleared her throat. "Take it down a notch, Ridley. That's not helping."

"Uh-uh. I'm tired of this hotshot here treating us like some bumbling amateurs. The fact is, Rico knew you were taking the kid to the clinic, and you can't blame that one on us, can you? It was a leak on your end, if you'd engage your brain for a minute."

Barnes shot him a warning look.

Marco shifted, the action uncorking a wave of pain in his side. He'd spent the ride over to the police station mulling over that exact detail. How did Rico know? How was he privy to their movements? Who was feeding him information?

"Mr. Quidel," Barnes said. "We need Candace Gallagher. She can put Rico away and end all of this violence. Rico did his dirty work in a clinic this time. Candace wasn't the only one in danger. There were doctors, nurses, patients. It could have been a catastrophe."

He'd thought about that, too, between the rounds of questioning. Rico's actions were getting desperate. *Rico's out of control. He's gonna bring us all down.* Marco had thought Champ was trying to skirt the blame, saying that, but maybe there really was unrest in the Pack about Rico's actions.

His hands ached, trembling slightly from the excruciating effort of keeping Candace from falling. He put them under the table.

"You understand better than anyone how bad this guy is," Barnes was saying.

Marco recalled Candace slipping slowly from his grasp as she dangled from the fire escape. Oh, yeah. He knew. "I understand your position," he said, "and she will be contacting you. But she needs her family right now so you're going to have to give her time." He stood slowly, trying to keep the groan of pain inside. "If we're all done here, I'd like to leave now."

Barnes gave him a resigned nod. "All right. She must call us. Soon. Tell her."

Ridley didn't stand as Marco trudged for the door. "Your pride is gonna get her killed, you know," he muttered.

"Like I said, this isn't about my pride."

"Yeah? Then what is it? Guy trying to save his lady love?"

Marco's temper blazed hot. "Doing my job."

"Your *job* is running a private investigation office. Following cheating husbands and chasing down stolen pets." Derision simmered in his words. "Don't get confused and think you're still a navy hero because you're not. You're a civilian, Quidel."

Marco continued out the door, his gut knotted tight. He stopped to fire off a question. "The other witness. Do you have him in protective custody?"

A quick tightening of the cop's mouth told the truth.

"What happened, Ridley?"

Ridley stared at the faded bulletins tacked to the wall.

"What happened?" Marco repeated.

Ridley glared at him. "He's dead, and a cop wounded. He was being transferred to another location and there was a drive-by shooting."

It was so quiet he could hear the ticking of the clock high on the chipped stucco wall. "So Candace Gallagher is the only chance you have to bring down Rico."

"Yeah."

Marco knew in that moment he would take down Jay Rico on his own, no matter what. In order to do it, he might need to separate from the Gallaghers, for their protection, but if the cops couldn't do it, he would have no other choice. The thought added to his pain.

He took the stairs slowly, suddenly feeling much older than his years as the discomfort attacked his every joint.

Candace was the only person who could destroy Jay Rico.

And Rico knew it.

The sun chased away the storm by midafternoon. Candace knew she should be calling the police, but she simply couldn't make herself do it. She was sore and exhausted, with frequent flashbacks leaving her in a strange state of inertia, so instead of contacting the cops, she accompanied Tracy and Bear to the beach with JeanBeth, Lon and Marco. Perhaps the buttery sunlight would drive away the chill that seemed to have penetrated deep into her pores.

Her wrists ached, but the pain reliever Dan had brought with him dulled the edge of the discomfort. He'd also brought the antibiotics for Tracy that Dr. Finch prescribed after the strep culture came back positive, and assured her that a quick beach excursion would be safe. Marco and Dev had already scoured every inch of beach and tree line. Even so, Dev headed for a position down the road so he could radio Marco at the first sign of danger.

Candace sat on the remains of a fallen tree and watched Tracy making what appeared to be a sand volcano with her grandma. They had a lively conversation about the difference between lava and magma. Lon assigned himself to the job of retrieving rocks to decorate the construction. He went cheerfully about his mission, but continually scanned the beach. She caught a glimpse of the gun tucked in a holster under his arm.

The wind whipped Candace's hair into a wild tangle, the air still cooler than usual after the passing storm. She felt a presence behind her.

Marco handed her the red scarf she usually kept crammed in her jacket pocket.

"You left it in the kitchen. Thought you might need it."

She twined it around her hair and tied back the curly mop. "Thank you."

There were so many things she wanted to say, but where to begin? Gratitude, she figured, was usually the best starting point.

"Thank you for saving me from falling."

He looked away. "Sorry it happened in the first place."

"Your ribs must hurt, and your arms. Bad?"

He shrugged. "You?"

"I think I'll recover." She held out her wrists. He took one gently in his big hand and skimmed an index finger over the bruises. The gesture made little sparks trail up and down her spine, so she eased herself from his grasp.

"Let me know if you need anything lifted. I'll take care of it. Don't want to strain your wrists any further."

The silence between them grew and so did the emotions bubbling inside her. "Marco," she said, after taking a deep breath, "I can't do this anymore."

He watched her carefully, waiting, always so patient with her.

"I'm trapped between two heroes," she said, twisting a sliver of tree bark between her fingers.

He frowned, still quiet as she spooled out the words.

"Rick was a marine, rock solid, larger than life. He sacrificed himself to save his team. That's a type of courage that's hard to live up to. And then there's you, Marco Quidel. Loyal, sometimes arrogant, but with courage enough to stand against Rico and put your life at risk to take him down." She looked at him then, the watery sunlight playing across his tanned skin, his full lips pursed in thought. "I wanted to have that kind of courage, to live up to Rick's legacy and be just as strong as you are, but I can't."

"You're plenty strong, Candace. You held on there, up

on that fire escape." He cleared his throat. "No one stronger than you."

"You're going to change your mind when you hear what I've decided."

He shook his head. "I will never change my mind about you."

Her lips trembled. "I'm going to quit, Marco. I cannot risk Tracy's life to put away Jay Rico. Justice is important to me, but not as important as she is."

Candace waited for him to speak, but he didn't.

"I am going to tell the police I won't testify, not about Kevin Tooley and not about what happened at the clinic."

He nodded.

"I know the judge can jail me for not testifying, but I'm willing to take the risk. It's over for me and Tracy."

"I understand."

"Do you?" She sought for signs of disappointment in his eyes, but found none. "I feel so guilty and ashamed. Rick…" Tears blurred her vision.

Marco crouched down next to her with a soft groan, craning his head to look into her eyes. His voice was soft when he spoke. "Candace, Rick would be proud of your decision, no question."

Would he be proud of her for quitting? A harder question was what he would think of the emotions she felt when she looked at Marco, feelings that had far exceeded the bounds of friendship.

"He would respect how hard you've fought and your commitment to Tracy." He cleared his throat. "And I could never be anything but proud of you." The softness in that hardened soldier's face awakened such a flood of tenderness that she reached up and cupped his cheeks with her hands. His eyes closed for a moment at the caress, before they flickered open again. The connection held them together, strengthened by their trauma, deepened by the years they'd enjoyed as the best of friends. His warmth pushed away the cold, and she desperately wanted to stay there, close to Marco.

What was she doing? The guilt hit with the force of a hammer blow. She let her hands drop to her sides and she stood. "Thank you for understanding, Marco."

"You made the right call for your family," he said, straightening with effort.

Her family. A family that did not include him. Did it? She looked out at the rolling waves of the Pacific, inching closer to the impressive sand volcano. The notion of resuming a normal life after the whole debacle tantalized her. Tracy would be thrilled to get back to school, and Candace to the comfort of car pools, swim meets and daily walks on the shore. Maybe she would take a break from the private investigation firm until she had better control of her emotions, especially around Marco. Things would be all business between them.

"I heard the other witness was killed," she said. "So Rico will get away with it all."

"No."

She jerked to face him. "Marco, it's over. He wins, that's all."

"It's over for you and Tracy."

She took him by the shoulders and his hands went reflexively to her waist. "For all of us."

He didn't answer.

She clutched his shirt. "Please tell me you won't go after Rico. He'll kill you without a second thought."

The trace of a smile tugged at the corner of Marco's mouth. "Good guys always win, remember?"

Anger flashed through her and she wanted to shake this stubborn wall of a man. "No, they don't," she snapped. "Stop staying that. Rick died with countless other good men and women. They didn't win. They didn't get to come home." Tears welled in her eyes.

"Rick had a family and a woman who adored him, and a cause he believed in. He knew his final destination. That's winning."

She felt the anger drain out of her, and dropped her forehead to his chest. "But Marco, it's so hard to be the one left behind."

His arm went around her, pulling her close. "I know, honey."

She stayed in the basket of his arms, protected from the wind and soothed by the steady beat of his heart. "I won't let you go after Rico," she mumbled into his chest. His silence made her pull away, and she glared at him full on, fury pouring out of her. "Did you hear me? This is your pride talking, because he's beaten you, beaten us. It's a stupid reason to go and get yourself killed."

He remained silent.

"And I don't want Pacific Coast Investigations involved, either." She flung the words at him.

"It won't be."

She stared, trying to read his thoughts. "What do you mean?"

"I'm going to leave the agency."

Shock stripped her of a response. She realized she'd stopped breathing. "What are you saying?"

"I'm leaving PCI to put some distance between us. When I bring Rico down, he won't even see it coming and if things get ugly he won't be able to retaliate against you or your family."

Desperation crept from her stomach into her chest. "This isn't the way."

"It's the only way." Marco spoke with a perfect calm that belied the ferocity of his words. "Jay Rico will go to jail if it takes me the rest of my life."

She tried to shake him, but he was immovable. “No,” she whispered.

“He will be punished for what he did to you.”

The hard, flat metal of Marco’s eyes chilled her. Now it was a mission for him and he wouldn’t stop until he’d succeeded or died trying. “I don’t want you hurt, not another man that I…” *That I love?* She swallowed. “Don’t get hurt for me. I don’t need vengeance.”

“I will bring him down.” His voice wasn’t loud, but the phrase might as well have been shouted over the roaring surf. He turned back toward the house and Candace knew with a flood of fear that she was powerless to change his mind.

Back inside, she heard her cell phone buzz, alerting her about a text with an attached picture. She didn’t recognize the sender’s number. Something prickled deep down as she looked at the tiny image. It was a shot of her mother and Lon, taken through the front window of JeanBeth’s house. Her stomach clenched into a ball. Another picture followed, of Angela buying coffee at a Coronado shop, Dan holding her hand. Then there was a shot of Donna and Brent running together on the beach.

Candace was so frightened she could hardly read the message.

You will meet me at the following location or they will all die. J.R.

Jay Rico had gotten her cell phone number somehow. Her heart beat a terrified rhythm.

It was plain crazy for her to go and meet Jay Rico.

But what other choice did she have?

Meet me…or they will all die.

One final image followed, of Marco getting out of his truck with Bear right behind him.

Rock and a hard place.

SIXTEEN

Marco wasn't surprised that after Candace's decision not to testify was forwarded by the police to the district attorney, the DA pushed hard for her to reconsider. If she didn't, the DA's case would disintegrate. He told her he'd contact her again on Monday for her final decision. Marco knew she'd already made it.

In her shoes, he half wished he was the kind of person who would have made the same choice, but Candace was right. Pride wouldn't have let him. For Marco, losing to Jay Rico stung like a swarm of hornets. He'd fought terrorists all over the world, glorified bullies with weapons who silenced their victims through intimidation, and now, right here on US soil, he'd let Rico terrorize Candace into submission. It galled him through his morning workout, and though he tried desperately to clear his mind and focus on his Bible reading, peace would not come.

The only thing that eased the discomfort was the knowledge that he would get Jay Rico in the end. Candace might have bought herself time by agreeing not to testify, but Rico was a man who held on to grudges, and Marco would never fully believe she was safe until the thug was imprisoned for life. It would cost Marco leaving Pacific Coast Investigations, leaving Candace, but he was certain it was the only way. He couldn't let go of his need for vengeance, which would paint him as a target—him and anyone close to him.

He flashed on Candace, hanging there, slipping slowly from his grasp, brown eyes so full of a life left to be lived.

There's another reason you're leaving. That deep-down ache for Candace that he would not allow to the forefront. Not ever.

Dev cleared his throat, standing in the doorway of the kitchen. "I heard she's not going to testify."

"Yeah."

"So we're pulling out?"

"Looks that way. Gonna push for Candace and Tracy to stay for a while, to be sure Rico's got the message, but…"

"But Gumdrop's already packed."

He sighed. "Yeah."

Dev stroked his puff of beard.

"What?"

"You aren't going to let it go, the thing with Rico. It's too personal."

Marco said nothing.

"Gonna go lone wolf?"

Still he remained silent, which answered as well as any words could have.

Dev fingered the spot on his forehead that was now a yellowing bruise. "My unit is shipping out in three days, but if I'm in the States whenever it goes down, I got your back."

"Thanks, Dev."

Dev's eyes were thoughtful. "Rico's gonna rue the day he crossed you."

"He's going to rue the day he threatened Candace."

Dev cocked his head. "But you know what I'm thinking?"

"Do I want to know?"

"Probably not."

Marco sighed. "You're going to tell me anyway, so let's get it over with."

"If you had to give up on Rico to be a part of their lives—" he jerked a thumb in the direction of Candace and Tracy's rooms "—might be worth taking the loss for your girls."

It's not a choice, Marco wanted to say. *Rico will always be a threat. And they will never be my girls.*

He stared at his hands. Was it that obvious that his feelings for Candace had gone way beyond friendship? He opened his mouth to say he didn't need any advice, but Dev had already returned to their sleeping quarters.

Marco sat for a while, before it sank in that something felt off. The ramshackle house was too quiet. Angela had driven Brent back to the office and would return afterward. Perhaps Candace was napping? He trotted upstairs, to find Tracy watching a show on her iPad, Bear snoring at her feet.

"Feeling better, half pint?"

"Uh-huh." Tracy smiled. "Mommy says we're going home soon. Maybe I'll get to be in the play, after all."

"Where is your mom?"

"She said she had to go out."

He felt a twinge. "Out where?"

"To deliver a message. She borrowed Auntie Donna's van, I think."

His thoughts felt sluggish. Donna had driven back in Brent's car and Candace had borrowed the van she'd left behind. To deliver a message.

A terrifying conclusion leaped into his head. Was she going to tell Jay Rico personally that she wouldn't testify, and try to end things once and for all? That would be sheer lunacy. Panic settled into Marco's gut. What was she thinking? In Jay Rico's world there would be no such thing as forgive and forget.

He recalled their conversation before Rico fired five rounds at Candace through the truck's windshield.

"If Candace Gallagher tries to testify, she's going to die."

Would the threat still hold even if she didn't? A cold sweat bathed his forehead.

Forcing a calm expression, he knelt next to Tracy. "When did she leave?"

"I don't know."

"Can you make a guess?"

"When my show started, and it's halfway done."

So fifteen minutes. Twenty maybe?

"Okay." He whirled toward the door.

"When are we going home, Unco?" Tracy called.

He didn't take the time to answer. Downstairs, he called Candace's cell.

Pick up, pick up, he willed. There was no answer. He sent a text.

Do not do this.

No reply.

He tried to order his thoughts. Where would she expect to find Rico? She couldn't very well drive around the seedier streets of Southern California asking for the man.

He tried her cell again. No answer.

He called for Dev, who came instantly.

"I have to go find her," he said, after filling Dev in. "Taking your bike."

"Orders?"

"Stay here with Tracy."

Dev didn't like it. Marco read that in his face. But there was no one else. "If something goes wrong, call in Lon and get Tracy out."

Dev gave him a thumbs-up. "Watch your back, Chief."

He hadn't felt fear before in the way he did at that moment and it nearly paralyzed him. "Not the spirit of fear," he hissed to himself. "That's not from God."

He called the office and got Donna on the third ring.

"I need you to ping Candace's cell phone. I have to know where she is right now."

To her credit, he heard her fingers clicking on the keys before she asked the question. "What's wrong?"

"She's gone to meet Rico."

Donna gasped. "Why would she do that?"

Why?

"I don't know yet. Do you have the location?"

"Got it," she said, giving him an address a mile from the Iron Works Gym. "Should I call the police?"

If Rico got a whiff of cops, even the suspicion that Candace was leading the police to his location, she'd be dead. He gripped the phone in a stranglehold.

"Negative."

"Marco…" Donna said.

"Can't talk anymore. Gotta go."

He clicked off and gunned the motorcycle to life, praying he wouldn't be too late.

Candace sat in the shade of a tattered sidewalk umbrella outside a deli advertising the world's largest pastrami sandwich. She kept her back to the storefront, eyeing the flux of customers crowding in and out, enjoying fat sandwiches filled with meat and all the fixings. Cigarette butts littered the cement, and she tried not to breathe in the smoke from the cluster of men leaning on the brick wall a few feet away. Were they Rico's guys? They seemed uninterested in her. She'd made herself as inconspicuous as possible, dressed in jeans and a faded T-shirt, her hair captured more or less in a messy ponytail.

Before she'd sneaked out of the beach house, she'd thought and prayed long and hard about whether it was the right thing to do. She knew in the deepest part of her heart that her family's only chance at safety would be for her to obey Rico's summons, meet with him face-to-face and convince him she'd given up. It was what his ego demanded—her utter defeat and surrender. But the other possible scenario was that the whole meeting was a trap and she was about to be killed. She blinked away the memories of the texted pictures.

Her family.

Her life.

Her decision, for better or worse. Further, she understood that Marco would not be able to stand by and let her do it.

A heavyset man wearing a blue bandanna bumped her table.

She straightened, one hand in her purse on the trigger of her pepper spray. The stuff would be a paltry defense if Rico had his people drive by and gun her down like they had the boy at the gas station. The heavyset man mumbled an apology and moved on.

She recalled Kevin Tooley's face, his mouth tight and twisted with hatred. He would go free, free to kill again, to murder someone else's child. Worse yet, he would revel in the knowledge that his gang had triumphed over the justice system. Pack justice had prevailed. It galled her.

Marco was wrong. The good guys didn't always win.

A familiar blonde woman dropped into the chair next to her, sporting the same heavy eye makeup and hostile look she'd had in the ladies' room at the courthouse. Candace gripped the pepper spray again.

"Where's Rico?" she asked.

The blonde surveyed the customers slowly before she answered. "Across the street at the park. You're going to go there."

"We were supposed to meet here."

She flicked an impatient hand. "You go where he tells you if you want to talk to him."

"Why not here?"

She eyed the patrons nearby under the pretense of fixing her hair. "A man like him has enemies."

"I read that Rico's been moving in on another gang's territory. Is he worried about retaliation?"

Her eyes narrowed to slits. "That's not your business."

"It is, if you're expecting trouble."

"My only trouble right now is you."

"I..."

The girl checked her cell phone. "Across the street in five minutes. If you don't show, that would be your mistake." She pocketed her phone. "You've got plenty to lose, don't you? If there's a cop or anyone at all following you..."

"There isn't."

"You'd better hope so for your family's sake." She walked away, crossing the street and heading for the cluster of trees at the end of the park.

Candace let go of the pepper spray and tried to squeeze her hands together to stop them from trembling. Jay Rico might be luring her to a quieter location where he could kill her without witnesses.

Marco would tell her she was being reckless, not thinking clearly, and he would probably be right.

Her only chance was to convince Rico that she would never testify against him or any of the Pack. The notion stung. *Get this done*, she told herself firmly. *Protect your family and give Tracy back the future she deserves, the one her father envisioned for her.*

"I'm doing everything I can, Rick," she whispered.

After five painful minutes, she clutched her purse to her side and forced her shaky legs to carry her across the boulevard to a grassy stretch that curved along the sidewalk. Trees shaded the area and a small section of sand was home to an unoccupied set of swings.

She saw no sign of the blonde girl. A couple sat together on a park bench about twenty feet from the trees, sharing a pair of earbuds, probably listening to some music. They might hear her if she screamed, if she actually had time to scream. The memory of the switchblade at her throat made her swallow hard.

Walking slowly toward the trees, she wondered if Rico's guys were watching her, closing in from behind. Jerking a quick look back, she saw no one.

A shadow appeared at the edge of the grove. Focusing, she found Jay Rico leaning against a broad trunk, eyes hidden behind sunglasses. He was wearing a short-sleeved shirt, faded jeans and ankle boots, his thumbs hooked in his belt loops as he slouched there. He scanned behind her, along the nearby street, as she prodded herself forward to meet him.

His lips curved into a cruel line, and she had no doubt he'd enjoyed every minute of the torture he'd inflicted on her earlier.

She forced down the rage that threatened to spill out. *Just get it over with.* "You don't need to hurt my family. I'm not going to testify about Kevin Tooley or anything else."

His sunglasses didn't allow her to pick up any expression, but a look of satisfaction slowly crept across his face. "So I heard, but I wanted to look into your eyes when you said it. You've decided that justice isn't worth the price?"

Candace took a slow breath in and out before she answered. "You are a thug and you deserve to be punished along with Kevin Tooley, but I'm not going to risk my daughter's safety or anyone else's."

"So I guess your high-and-mighty sense of what's right and wrong isn't so cut-and-dried, after all. Fear trumps everything."

No, love does, she wanted to say, but there was no point in it. She exhaled slowly. "Anyway, that's it."

She waited, but he remained silent. Was he telling the truth—that he just needed to see her in person to be convinced she wouldn't testify? Had he sent the terrifying pictures just to torture her for his own twisted enjoyment?

"You got what you wanted. Leave us alone." She turned to go.

"What about the sailor?"

"Pardon?"

"Your sailor man, Popeye. Is he willing to let it go, too? He running scared enough to retreat?"

Oh, how Rico underestimated Marco Quidel. "Yes. As a matter of fact, he's leaving Pacific Coast Investigations."

Rico laughed. "That right? Too bad. I was gonna enjoy killing him."

"Is that how you handle everyone who threatens you?"

"That's how I keep what I got. If your enemies ain't scared of you, you're gonna lose everything."

What a way to live, she thought, *binding people to you through fear instead of love.* "I'm no longer a threat to you." She started to walk away.

"But maybe I don't trust you and the sailor," Rico said, suddenly behind her.

She stopped and prickles erupted on her spine as she felt the cold metal of a gun pressed to the base of her skull.

"I got lots of enemies, baby. Lots of people gunning for me. That's the price of being the lead dog. Could be that you'll change your mind down the road and come gunning for me, too."

Her mouth was dry as sand. "I won't."

He pressed the gun harder, sending sparks of pain through her skull. "But why should I trust you?"

"Because killing me would net you even more enemies," she told him, forcing herself not to flinch. "The police, my family."

His breath was hot against her neck as he spoke. "No one will see me do it, so the police will be impotent. As for your family..." He moved the gun up and down her neck in a grotesque caress. "They won't come after me because they have too much to lose. Love can make you weak, if you let it."

Her mind scrambled for what to say to keep him from shooting her. She recalled their first conversation.

You remind me of a woman I knew. Spirited and feisty.

"Did your girl make you weak when she betrayed you?"

"Quiet," he snapped, pressing so hard with the gun that Candace's eyes teared up.

Her whole body was shaking now. "You couldn't own her and she left, isn't that what happened?"

"Jay," a voice screamed. It was the blonde from the deli. "Look out! They're coming. They're—"

Her words were cut off as a dark SUV rocketed across the parking lot and jumped the curb, shuddering over the expanse of grass. The driver cranked the wheel until the car was parallel to the row of trees. The passenger window slid down and an automatic weapon spat bullets in a deadly stream. The woman pitched over, onto her back.

SEVENTEEN

Marco heard the screams as he roared into the parking lot. A black SUV, vomiting gunfire, churned toward the trees, kicking up chunks of sod and grit. The couple who had been occupying a nearby park bench fled hand in hand from the park, faces frozen in terror.

A body lay prone on the ground in the shadows, a woman's slender frame.

His stomach knotted into a cold fist. The car shot past the trees and headed away. Marco leaped from the bike and ran to the fallen woman, turning her over as gently as he could.

Blond hair, tight jeans, heavy makeup—the woman Candace had sprayed at the courthouse. Blood stained her stomach through her T-shirt, but it appeared to him that the bullets had skimmed her body rather than cutting through it, and she was breathing, her eyes beginning to open. He untied the jacket from her waist and pressed it to the wound, all the while scanning desperately for Candace.

"Candace," he yelled. There was no movement from under the trees. Had she doubled back out to the street? Or was she unable to respond?

The blonde groaned and tried to sit up.

"Stay still. You need an ambulance."

She batted at his arms. "Leave me alone."

"Press here, with your hand," he ordered, placing her palm on the makeshift bandage.

She did, moaning, tears streaking the black eyeliner down her cheeks in dark rivulets. Vulnerability peeped through the mask of gang girl toughness and he glimpsed the long-ago child she must have been. "Am I gonna die?" she whispered.

"No, not if you keep the bleeding under control and we get you to a hospital."

The black SUV had made a sharp U-turn, returning for a second round of mayhem.

"Gotta get to cover," he barked. He started to drag her toward the relative safety of the trees, but she fought him, wriggling out of his grasp.

"I can't go with you. I have to help Rico."

Over her shoulder, he saw an Escalade approaching from the other direction, the two cars bearing down on each other in a deadly game of chicken.

"We're going to get caught in the cross fire," he snapped at her.

Again he tried to move her to shelter, and again she pushed him away, getting to her feet and half crawling, half running. This time he let her go, and sprinted toward the trees as the vehicles drew nearer. When the Escalade's windows rolled down, he was behind the trees. Bullets tore chunks out of the bark as the driver ground to a stop. A guy in the back of the Escalade laid down a screen of cover fire while the wounded girl leaped into the backseat.

The black SUV moved to intercept, firing wildly, flattening one of the Escalade's tires. Sound battered Marco's ears as he weaved in and out of the trees. Park visitors screamed and ran for safety or dropped to their knees, covering their heads.

"Candace!" he shouted over the roar of bullets and car engines. He didn't hear an answer as he swiped the sweat from his eyes, searching.

He yelled again, and her faint reply, "Here," was sweeter than music to his ears.

She was crouched in a ball at the foot of an oak, flecks

of splintered wood clinging to her hair. He flung himself to his knees. "Are you hit?"

She shook her head. "It's probably Rico's rivals, the Cliffs. They're trying to take over his territory."

"I—" His answer was drowned in an avalanche of noise. He pulled her to him as another fusillade of bullets plowed their own deadly pattern into the trees. Wishing he had his hands on some weaponry to force their retreat, or at least a set of body armor with which to swaddle Candace, Marco sheltered her body with his the best he could. When the shooting ended, they peered out from their feeble hiding place. He put together an escape route in his mind, but before he could tell her, she clutched his arm.

"Look."

Jay Rico broke from the shadows of the trees, running for the waiting Escalade.

An act of desperation and idiocy, Marco thought. "He's gonna get himself killed."

A fresh stream of gunfire erupted from the SUV.

Candace screamed as Rico, struck repeatedly in the chest, flew backward and fell to the ground.

There was nothing to be done, Candace finally concluded, after another hour had passed. The police had cordoned off the scene and questioned her and Marco and the two other eyewitnesses thoroughly. Candace told them why she'd gone to meet Jay Rico and how he'd been ambushed by a rival party. The police confirmed it was most likely the Cliffs.

"Things have been heating up with them," the cop said. "They didn't take it well when he tried to move in on their territory, and now word's out that Rico has some internal trouble in his organization."

"He's got more than that now," Marco said.

"Rico was shot," Candace added dully.

Marco nodded. "Multiple rounds to the chest. At that point the SUV retreated. Rico's guys hauled him into the backseat of the Escalade and they took off."

Ridley tapped a pencil. "So you believe Jay Rico is dead?"

"Probably," Marco said. "But I'll reserve judgment until I see a body."

Ridley sighed, looking suddenly much older. "All the blood, sweat and tears we've put in trying to nail this guy and it comes to this. What a colossal waste of time and resources."

Candace wondered if he would blame her for not accepting police custody at the beginning of the whole mess, but he didn't. She was so muddled she no longer knew what the smart decisions were. All she could hold on to was that it was done. Over. She believed Rico was dead and he would never threaten her and Tracy again. It should have made her feel a sense of relief. Instead she was filled with sorrow.

What a waste, indeed. A life of crime and violence ended in an inevitable hail of bullets. At least innocent bystanders had not been hurt, but there had to be a different way for it all to have turned out. She wanted to close her eyes and pray, but that would have to wait until the police interviews were complete and she could find a place to be alone.

Marco checked in with Dev, and Candace was reassured to hear that Tracy was happily beating Dev at checkers and he had prepared her a lunch of microwave popcorn and apple slices. At least it wasn't ice cream. Brent agreed to come and retrieve Donna's van.

As she climbed onto the back of the motorcycle, Candace was grateful for the excuse to hold Marco tight. Gripping his strong torso anchored her against the storm she'd just experienced. Wind whipped her hair under the helmet and she let the past few weeks unroll in her memory, one hideous moment after the next. The recollections felt surreal—the grenade thrown through her kitchen window, the ambush near the freeway where she'd first met Rico face-to-face, her fingers gripping the fire escape railing at the clinic.

Climb up on the edge and jump...

She squeezed her eyes shut. *"It's done, Candace. You don't have to think about it anymore, ever again."*

But there was one niggling detail, one piece of the puzzle, that refused to go quietly back into the box. She should let it go, but the private investigator in her would not be silent.

"Marco," she called over the wind, as they passed a crowded coffee shop. "Can we stop there?"

He pulled into the small parking lot, squeezed into a space, and they went inside.

"You need a little time before you face everybody?" he asked.

She smiled. "No, but that's very nice of you to ask."

He lifted a shoulder. "I'm getting to be a real sensitive guy."

She laughed, amazed that it was possible she'd held on to her sense of humor through the last four months. "I know you really want to take me to task for going to meet Rico without you."

A muscle in his jaw twitched. "It was ill advised, but there's no point in going over that right now. I understand, now that you've told me about the pictures he texted you."

"Thank you for that. I need a Wi-Fi connection to do some research."

He frowned. "Presuming Rico is dead, aren't we...done with this case?"

"Just one more thing I want to know if I'm ever going to be able to put it all behind me."

His frown deepened. There was a scratch on his chin

from the dive under the trees, and the stiffness in his movements told her he was still in pain from preventing her fall at the clinic. The four months had been an excruciating journey for him, also, physically and mentally.

She wanted to touch, to smooth away the worry lines that grooved his forehead.

"Please," she said. "I need to do this."

The copper flecks sparked in his eyes. After a long moment he said, "After what you've endured, you deserve some closure."

She was grateful that he understood, respected her desire to end things on her own terms instead of ordering her to cease and desist as he would have done in the past. She put her fingers lightly to his chest, surprised that they had finally stopped shaking after what she'd just experienced.

"Maybe you really are turning into a sensitive guy," she teased softly.

"Don't let it get around." He looked at her fingers, his own hands moving a fraction as if he wanted to reach up and touch her, but he didn't.

"I just need one minute…" She paused. "And a vanilla latte?" she suggested hopefully.

He rolled his eyes and groaned. "I've been reduced to the coffee guy. That hurts."

"Coffee Guy is a fabulous nickname. What was your nickname in your SEAL days, by the way? All this trauma hasn't made me forget. I haven't had a chance to pry it out of Dev yet."

"And you never will." Muttering, but with a small smile visible, Marco turned and went to buy her a coffee.

The hot sweet brew soothed her, the touch of normalcy helping her temporarily put aside what had just happened to her, and to Jay Rico. Ten minutes of surfing and she had the answer she was looking for.

"Dr. Finch said Yolanda's mother was unable to come

for her after she was run down by the car. I used the PCI resources and I found her. Anna Tooley is still alive. She rents an apartment about forty-five minutes from here."

Marco sipped from his bottle of water. "And we need this information why?"

"I can't explain it exactly, but I have to know more about what happened to Yolanda Tooley. It somehow has a bearing on Kevin Tooley. I just need to know."

"Private eye instinct?"

"Maybe. Are you willing to make a stop there before we go back? Since we're going home soon and…and you're still planning on leaving PCI, I guess this is our last case together."

It hurt to say it and Marco's face was unreadable. She didn't find the regret or hesitation she was hoping for. He stared at his hands. "Yes."

"You are convinced Rico's not dead, aren't you? But even if he survived, there's no reason for him to come after me again. No trial."

"If there's the slightest chance that he survived, I need to pursue that. Just like you're pursuing this thing about Kevin Tooley's mother."

"Is this your ego talking?"

He shrugged. "Maybe. Doesn't matter. I'm going to find him."

"Fine. If you're so determined, then stay with PCI and we'll work the case together."

He looked away. "I'm going to move on. I'll have more flexibility to act away from the agency, and you've got Brent and Dan. Plenty of help. It's the right time for me to go."

Pain shot through her heart. Why should he second-guess his decision to leave, anyway? He'd joined the company only as a favor to her father and a means to keep an eye on the Gallagher women, his adopted family. Now they were all grown and married, or headed that way, with men to watch over them.

And now that this case it almost over, you're settled, too, she reminded herself.

But she didn't feel settled just then.

Marco guided her out the door with a hand on the small of her back. Maybe meeting Anna Tooley would let her put things to rest and she could ease back into her life with Tracy and her memories of Rick.

Unless Rico wasn't really dead. Candace couldn't shake the feeling that somehow the case was not quite closed. The only lead they hadn't followed to the end was Rico's unusual protectiveness of Kevin Tooley, and she felt the answer lay just out of reach. Was that the root of her unease? Just a case unfinished? Or was it the knowledge that she would soon have to say goodbye to Marco?

Brushing the feelings aside, she climbed back onto the bike and crammed the helmet over her curls, wondering if the next stop would bring answers or simply more questions.

EIGHTEEN

It didn't matter what her reasons were, particularly. Marco was content to accompany Candace to Anna Tooley's apartment, though he wasn't convinced it would provide any further clarity. After nearly getting caught in the middle of a gang shootout, a quiet ride along city streets was good for their nerves, however. She needed to follow through and he was pleased to be the one standing next to her when she did it. He'd savor that privilege.

They arrived at a well-tended apartment building, not close to the beach but near enough that he could hear the crash of the distant waves. There was no front desk help, so they found Anna Tooley the old-fashioned way, by locating her initials on the stacked mailboxes.

"A.T., Unit 114, first floor," Marco read. He hurried to keep up with Candace, who was setting a quick pace. His body had not yet recovered from the earlier situation at the clinic. His muscles reminded him he wasn't a twenty-something anymore. As usual, he ignored them, and caught up with her when she knocked on the door. After several moments she knocked again.

The door was eventually opened by a young girl in a T-shirt and jeans, who looked them over with a suspicious eye.

"Yeah?"

"Hi," Candace said, introducing herself. "I'm looking for Anna Tooley. Is this her apartment?"

"It was."

"Was? Did she move?"

"Uh-uh," the girl said, chewing a piece of gum. "She died."

Candace let out a breath. "Oh no."

"When?" Marco said.

"Two days ago." She flicked a glance at him. "Who are you two, anyway? Family? Bill collectors?"

"No, we are investigators. We're looking into her daughter's death," Candace said.

The girl raised an eyebrow. "Yolanda died a long time ago. Got run over, I heard. Mrs. Tooley didn't like to talk about it 'cuz it made her cry."

"Are you family?" Candace asked.

"Nah. I work here at the apartments. I'm supposed to clean and help pack up. Her nephew was here yesterday, starting to box everything, but then he had to leave. Boss wants to rent out the unit as soon as he can." She blew out a breath. "Guy's got no love for anything but the dollar."

"Would it be okay if we took a quick look around?" Candace said.

The girl shook her head. "Mrs. Tooley was a nice lady. She used to bake cookies for me sometimes. I don't think it's right to let people paw through her stuff."

"We won't, I promise," Candace said. "We won't touch anything."

"I don't think so."

"Mrs. Tooley lost her daughter," Marco said, "and they never punished the person who killed her. Don't you think she would want us to keep looking for justice?"

Two more chews on the gum and the girl stepped aside and opened the door.

"Okay," she said. "Fifteen minutes and you don't touch a thing. I'm going to stay here and watch, too."

"Thank you," Candace said, stepping into the apartment.

He followed her into a tiny front room with an adjoining kitchen. Cardboard boxes were stacked on the sofa and the walls were bare of any adornment except for an old eight-by-ten photograph of a woman he recognized from his research as Yolanda Tooley. She was dark haired, with a confident grin that he liked. It was probably her high school graduation picture, so she was maybe eighteen. So much promise, then to be murdered by someone who hadn't even stopped.

He turned away.

Candace walked down the hall to the bedroom, which was no more than a closet-sized space, almost full due to the twin bed. He didn't want to squeeze his bulk in with Candace already there, so he stayed in the doorway.

She stopped to look at a dusty dome of glass, under which was a dried flower and Yolanda's funeral notice. He heard Candace pull in a long, shaky breath, then her body slumped, head bowed, and he realized she was fighting tears. The day had caught up with her, or maybe the whole month.

"Hey," he said softly, pressing forward in spite of the tight space. "Is this too much right now? We can go."

She turned and buried her face in his chest. "It's just that I know how she felt. I have the pressed flowers from Rick's funeral."

He didn't have words, so he rubbed circles on her back.

"They're just old flowers, dried up petals, but you hold on to them because they remind you of what you lost." She sniffed and looked up at him with tearstains on her face. "Why do I do that? Remember the sad things? Rick and I had so many amazing moments, so much happiness. Why can't I just remember the joy and be glad for it?"

Marco cradled her close. "Seems like joy always has a little pain mixed in here on earth. I've always thought..." He trailed off. "Never mind."

The tears gave her irises the shimmer of ocean water before a storm.

"Thought what?"

He felt suddenly uncomfortable under her gaze. "That God gives us only a taste of joy to show us what's ahead, to remind us He's got something better."

She stared at him, a wistful expression on her face. "He's given me plenty of joy, but sometimes I let the pain push it away." She looked again at the desiccated flower. "Anna's heart was broken. She lost her child. I think about Tracy…" The tears pooled again. "I'm not sure I could survive that."

She cried for a while, the tears soaking his shirtfront, every one precious to him. He didn't say anything, just held her and savored the moments spooling out between them.

The girl poked her head in. "Five more minutes and then you have to go. My boss is coming back and I don't want him to find out I let you in."

Marco let go of Candace and nodded. "Thanks."

The girl's look softened as she took in Candace's tears. "I think it's sad, too." After a second of hesitation she added, "In the top drawer there's an album that hasn't been packed yet. You can look at it if you want to." She retreated.

Candace opened the drawer and took out a small photo album of four-by-six-inch pictures, the pages brittle with age. She sat on the bed and he stood next to her, crammed against the wall in order to peer over her shoulder.

Moments of the Tooleys' lives unfolded before him, starting with a young Anna Tooley smiling on her wedding day next to a tall man with the same dark hair as Yolanda. Then came the baby pictures, first a boy, then a grinning, roly-poly little girl with her fingers in her mouth. Those snapshots gave way to various elementary and high school pictures. Following that series there was a gap, until the photo of Yolanda holding her own baby, Kevin. That one brought Marco up short. What had happened to get this chubby-cheeked infant to the point where he would gun down another human being at a gas station?

Marco considered what his own book might look like. A serious child, he'd been told he'd always been quiet but active, more at ease doing any kind of physical labor than staying still.

Fast-forward three and a half decades and he was a battle-hardened ex-soldier, and the softest, sweetest part of his world was sitting at his side. He craved more than anything to hang on to the moment, to keep her there beside him, the woman who made him try to be patient, sensitive, humble, compassionate. Candace Gallagher, the best part of his world.

She is not yours and never will be, his heart reminded him in brutal fashion.

He looked again at Anna's book. She'd lost her husband, her daughter, and then her grandson to jail. Joy and pain were on display before them in the aging photos. Joy and pain.

The very last page held one more photo, torn at the corner. In it, Anna posed with Yolanda, both smiling at the toddler in the younger woman's arms. The man standing next to Yolanda had his hand draped playfully over her shoulders with the affection of a sibling. Her brother, the man who must have raised Kevin after she died…

Marco looked closer, incredulous.

Candace stared in horror.

"I can't believe it," she whispered.

He took the photo album from her hands and returned it to the drawer before they hurried from the room.

"Did you find something?" the girl called.

"Oh, yeah," Marco said grimly. "We sure did."

Candace made sure she got into the PCI office a step before Marco. He'd been dangerously tense all the way back to Coronado and she knew his anger was rising from a simmer to a full boil.

Betrayed.

They'd all been betrayed and nearly killed, and Marco was not a person to take that kind of thing calmly. Her own hands were shaking as they burst into the office.

They found Baxter, the office custodian, emptying the recycle bin in the main office, where Donna was on the phone. JeanBeth poked her head out of the conference room at their arrival, Lon next to her, carrying a carton of copy paper which he immediately put down as he took in Marco and Candace's expressions.

Marco rounded on Baxter. "You've been informing Jay Rico all along, haven't you?"

Donna hung up and shot to her feet. "What's going on?"

Baxter started. "I don't know what you're talking about."

"Yes, you do," Marco snapped. "You're Kevin Tooley's uncle. You got the job here shortly after Kevin was arrested, and you've been feeding info to Rico about our every move so he could terrorize Candace out of testifying."

"No, I would never—"

"You can't lie your way out of this one," Marco said, "so save the excuses. You listened in on the phone call about the courthouse, and when Dr. Dan was telling us about the clinic. You fed all that to your pal Jay Rico and it almost got Candace killed."

Baxter suddenly came alive, mouth twisted in anger. "Jay Rico is not my pal. I had no choice. I was trying to keep Kevin out of prison."

"Kevin deserves to be in prison," Marco shouted, slamming his hand onto the desktop. "He's a murderer, or doesn't that matter to you?"

Candace put a calming hand on Marco's wrist, feeling his thundering pulse. "Let him talk," she said quietly.

Marco clamped his jaw so tight she could see the vein jumping as he worked for control. Hands fisted on his hips, he stayed silent.

"Kevin wasn't a bad kid," Baxter said. "He was a good boy, a happy boy, until his mother was killed and then everything unraveled. Mom and I did our best, but we lost control." He rubbed his chin. "There was trouble in school, with the cops, everywhere, and we couldn't pull him out."

Candace thought the pain in Baxter's eyes was too real to be faked, but then he'd been lying to them from the start. "Go on."

"I almost couldn't go through with it when I snooped in the desks to find Candace's cell phone number to give to Rico. It felt like the last straw. I wanted to tell you the whole time but…" He heaved out a breath. "I didn't want anyone to be hurt, and I'm sorry for what I did. I just didn't see any other way to keep Kevin out of prison."

"Tell us about him," Candace said.

Baxter seemed to age before their eyes. "He wasn't even thirteen when the Pack started trying to pull him in. He loved it, the feeling of power, the family he was cheated out of. They gave him small jobs, money…made him feel important. And Jay Rico…" Baxter's expression hardened into hatred. "He made it his personal mission to ensnare Kevin. Kevin thought Rico was a superhero or something. Nothing my mom and I could say made the slightest difference. We lost him to the Pack and to Jay Rico before he was even fifteen years old."

The last piece of the puzzle fell into place. "Baxter, who is Kevin's father?"

He blinked and rubbed a hand over the back of his neck. "I don't know. Yolanda got pregnant while she was in high school and wouldn't name the father no matter how hard we pressed her."

Candace shook her head. "I'm sure most of that is true, but you know who the father is, don't you?"

He remained silent.

"You owe her the truth," Marco said, "after what you've done. She almost died."

He exhaled. "Rico started seeing Yolanda before he dropped out of high school. We tried everything to keep them apart, because Rico was already deep into the gang thing, but she loved him, or so she thought. They stayed together for two years."

Rico's words came back to her.

But she betrayed me. I decided a long time ago that no one gets to do that, so I didn't have a choice. You gotta draw the battle lines in your life, you know?

Candace let out a sigh. "He abused her?"

"Yeah," he said bitterly, "and all the while she made excuses for him. 'Oh, he's gonna change, Bax. He's just got a hot temper, Bax.' Even when he would hurt her, imagining she was interested in another man, she'd always forgive him. But she didn't walk away until it was too late."

"So you're saying…" Donna prodded.

"That Jay Rico ran her down with the car," he finished. "I never had any proof. It wouldn't have mattered, anyway. Rico was untouchable. Any of his guys would provide him an alibi."

"And Kevin doesn't know about the murder?" Donna asked.

Baxter shook his head.

"Or that Jay Rico was his father?" Candace said.

"No. Rico kept it secret that he was even involved with Yolanda, and he made her promise not to tell Kevin until he was older. I don't know why. He told her it was because he had a lot of enemies."

"It's the truth," Marco said. "Best way to get to someone is through their loved ones."

"We meant to tell him, someday, but it just never happened. But it doesn't matter anymore. Word on the street is that Rico's dead, shot down by the Cliffs, and Yolanda will never have justice. And Kevin doesn't even know his hero is the one who murdered his mother." Baxter's mouth shut in a tight line. "So what happens now? To me."

Marco was about to answer, but Candace cut him off. "Nothing. You go, leave this office and try to be an uncle to Kevin if he'll let you."

"After you lied to me?" a voice said from the office doorway.

Candace jerked in surprise. Marco leaped forward, standing between her and Kevin Tooley.

NINETEEN

In one fluid motion, Lon swept JeanBeth behind him and moved to flank Tooley. Marco saw no sign of a weapon tucked into the kid's baggy pants or under his T-shirt, but that didn't ease his mind. "Get out," he snapped.

"I did," Tooley said. "This morning. Strolled right out of jail after the case was dismissed." His gray eyes swept everybody in the room. Waiting to make a move?

Try it, kid. It will be the last one you ever make.

"I understand I got out of jail because this chick here isn't gonna testify." He stared at Candace.

"That's not a respectful term," Lon said. His tone was mild and his posture outwardly relaxed, but Marco knew otherwise.

Kevin shot him a look of disdain. "And I come to Coronado to make sure that's the straight answer and I find dear Uncle Bax here telling my life story." The cords in his neck were taut with rage. "Is it true, then, Uncle Bax? Jay Rico is my father, and he killed my mom?"

Baxter swallowed. "I'm sorry."

"Sorry doesn't quite cut it." Tooley's voice sounded constricted, as if somebody had him by the throat. "You've been lying to me, along with Grandma and Rico and everyone else."

"We didn't tell you because we wanted to protect you. Rico was right about that part. Anyone close to him has a target painted on his back."

His tone was bitter. "Jay Rico is the biggest liar of the

bunch. You know, I always wondered why he took such an interest in me. I actually thought he figured I was special."

"It doesn't matter now, Kev," Baxter said, taking a step toward him. "Jay Rico is dead, and you're out of jail. You're young, you can start over."

Kevin laughed. "Oh yeah. That's a great speech. You should write that down. I've got my whole life ahead of me, right?"

Marco edged forward. "Your family mess is not our concern. The trial is over, and the Gallaghers are out. We have no more business between us anymore, so I'm going to ask you again to leave and not come back."

Kevin's chin went up, fists balled.

Marco stayed loose and brought his hands up ever so slightly.

Kevin's gaze flicked between Marco and Lon. Marco hadn't seen Lon move, but somehow he was closer, the half smile still on his face, but now one hand was in his pocket.

Donna had the phone receiver, fingers ready to dial 911.

"Okay," Kevin said after a pause. "I've got better things to do, anyway."

Marco, Lon and Donna didn't move. Kevin looked at his uncle. "I don't want to see you ever again."

Baxter flinched. "I've tried to raise you as best as I could. I'm your only family."

Kevin shook his head. "The Pack was my family."

"Kev..." Baxter said, reaching out to him.

"Nah, Bax. Too late."

If Rico was dead, it was indeed too late. But if he wasn't... Marco watched out the window as Kevin Tooley vanished around the corner.

Two weeks passed in slow motion. Candace struggled to adjust, but the passing days didn't bring to light any word on Rico from police sources or Marco's ruthless investigation efforts. Her nights were restless, more often than not finding her pacing the house in the wee hours, checking the locks and listening to music to soothe her nerves. The family consensus was that Rico was dead, though they still kept an ear to the ground via PCI channels.

Dev had deployed and Lon retreated to complete his recovery in solitude, though he still called JeanBeth once a week to discuss Bible study questions. Last Candace had heard, JeanBeth had convinced him to come to Thanksgiving dinner if he wasn't back to active duty by then. Candace suspected Lon would be receiving care packages from her on a regular basis when he did return to his SEAL duties.

Finally, she grudgingly allowed Tracy to return to school, though Candace still found herself driving by the campus when her anxiety got too high. She'd park on the street, roll down the window and just listen. The noise of the kids running and shouting on the playground eased her. It was the carefree, joyous cacophony of normal life—life as it should be.

There had been no further threats of any kind. Marco remained unconvinced, even though Kevin was a free man, his gang father presumed dead and Candace no threat to Rico any longer.

Though he'd endured Candace's constant badgering with good grace, Marco had at last agreed that she did not need a full-time bodyguard anymore. After a casual goodbye celebration at Candace's house on a Friday evening, Marco accepted tearful hugs from all the Gallagher women and a ride to the marina from Candace for him and Bear, since his truck was still being repaired. They pulled up at the parking area and Candace killed the motor. Marco and Bear got out. The water of San Diego Bay sparkled against the white hulls of the moored boats. "Where will you go?"

"I won't be too far."

He leaned in the passenger window, while Bear did a canine dance in his excitement to be back aboard the *Semper Fortis*. "Gonna check out some of my old contacts, see if Rico surfaces in Mexico."

"But you don't have to do that. The trial is dismissed. Rico's not a factor," she said, for what seemed like the hundredth time.

"He will always be a factor for me until I find him dead or alive. The office can't devote 24/7 to finding him, but I can, and that's what I'm going to do." He rubbed a hand across his chin. "I… I haven't protected you and Tracy, not well enough. Ridley was right about that."

"No, he wasn't. You've been our rock."

He looked at his feet. "It's the right time to go.

The moment stretched long and taut between them. She desperately did not want him to leave, nor did she want to face the constant tension and guilt she would feel if he stayed.

"Let me walk you to your boat, at least." She got out and they strolled toward the dock. Waves lapped softly against the wooden piers. They stayed there, wrapped by the sound of the surf and the gulls in search of their last evening meal.

"Marco…" she started. But what could she say? *I will be lost without you. You are the one person who makes me feel whole. And I cannot love you because the guilt of giving my heart to another man would crush my soul...* "Tracy is going to miss you around the office," she said. "And so am I."

He nodded. "I'll come back sometimes."

"I hope so." Her throat grew thick with unshed tears. "Kids grow so fast you might not recognize her the next time you visit."

"You have my cell number. Text me pictures."

"You are a wreck at using a cell. It took you three months to learn how to text when you got a new phone."

He laughed. "Steep learning curve, I know." He stopped and fished something out of his pocket. "I almost forgot. Can you give this to Tracy?"

Candace palmed the little pink rabbit with big blue eyes. "She's going to love it," she said, her voice wobbling. "It will join the rest of the rabbit family you made her."

"If she ever gets tired of rabbits, let me know."

"She won't. You've always been so good to her, worked so hard to make her—to make both of us—happy."

"It wasn't work," he said quietly, still looking out at his boat bobbing on the waves.

"Marco, if things were different—"

He cut her off. "You deserve happiness, Candace. I hope you find it." He moved close and wrapped her in a tight hug, pressing his cheek to her forehead. She held on, holding him, silently pouring out her sadness, her guilt, the fear that she was letting go of a man who meant everything to her and shouldn't.

He kissed the top of her head, stepped away and whistled for Bear. While Candace watched with a leaden heart, the two of them made their way to the *Semper Fortis* and climbed aboard. Bear looked back at her in confusion and barked as if to say, *Are we really leaving?*

Are you?

Candace watched him cast off. The *Semper Fortis* grew smaller and smaller until it was swallowed up by the growing darkness. It felt to Candace as if her heart was overcome with shadows, too.

The wind tickled her hair, and a shadow raced along the periphery of her vision as she walked back to her vehicle. She jerked to her right. No one was there except for a car idling at the far end of the parking area. It was dark, nondescript, with tinted rear windows. Was it her imagination, or did she see the driver look in her direction? It was too far away to see his face. She wanted to run to the dock and call Marco back, but she wouldn't allow paranoia to take over her life.

Whatever Marco wanted to believe, the most likely scenario was that Rico was dead.

"Dead," she repeated to herself. Saying it aloud almost dispelled the residual fear as she jogged to her car, leaped inside and locked the doors.

It was hard to pace the deck of the bobbing boat as he waited to hear from his source about a dark-haired stranger who'd arrived in Tijuana the previous evening with plenty of cash.

When his pacing finally elicited an irritable bark from Bear, Marco figured he'd walk into town, cell phone in his hand, Bear at his side sniffing every shrub and flower. On the way he made a mental list of what to do if his informant confirmed that the stranger was Rico. Getting into Mexico wasn't going to be a problem, but he'd have to acquire a weapon once he got there.

Bear sat at attention outside the entrance to a convenience store while Marco bought a case of water. He stopped to pay at the counter. The news was spooling out over the television. It annoyed him that there seemed to be televisions everywhere now, from gas stations to restaurants.

"Increased gang hostilities." The newscaster's phrase caught his attention. He handed over some bills and focused on the screen.

"Rival gangs, the Wolf Pack and the Cliffs, are apparently engaged in a turf war after the reported death of Pack leader Jay Rico. Though Rico's body has not been recovered, it's believed the altercation at Sand Dune Park on November 10 left him mortally wounded or dead. It is unclear who is second in command to Rico and the current skirmishes, which have left two dead and three wounded, may indicate the death knell of the Pack."

Marco shoved the change in his pocket and thanked the clerk, stepping away to hear the rest. There was a shot of some young men standing on a street corner, smoking cigarettes, pants sagging to their hips. The picture of innocence, he thought wryly.

The camera panned to one youth wearing Cliffs colors. "Nothing going on here, man," he said. Marco felt an electric shock go through him. Just behind the speaker, Kevin Tooley leaned against the wall, arms folded, a smirk on his face. So Tooley had left the Pack and joined up with their enemies. It shouldn't surprise Marco, with the future of the Pack in doubt. Though Tooley might just as likely have decided to jockey for leadership in the wake of his father's death. Perhaps the hatred he felt for Jay Rico for killing his mother prevented him from wanting anything to do with his old gang family.

Nothing unexpected there, Marco told himself as he left the shop. It didn't change a thing. Candace was safe in Coronado, away from the escalating gang violence, and even if Rico had somehow survived, she was no longer a threat to him.

But there was still no body recovered. That didn't mean anything, either. There were plenty of places to dispose of a body, especially in a city near the ocean. Or maybe Rico really had survived and was lying in a hospital bed somewhere, or had split town. Still, it didn't indicate any renewed threats to Candace and Tracy, since Kevin Tooley's case had been dismissed.

She's fine. Tracy's fine. Don't imagine trouble as an excuse to return because you miss them more than you could ever have imagined.

So if everything was fine, why were his nerves on edge?

His phone rang, and he answered. His contact greeted him in Spanish and cut to the chase. "It's not your guy here in Mexico."

Marco sighed. Another dead end. "Okay, man. Thanks."

After a moment, he dialed the number for his snitch at the Iron Works Gym.

"Yeah," the kid said. "Rico's locker was cleaned out sometime in the last week. We didn't know it happened 'cuz someone came and did it at night. Weird, huh?"

Marco thanked him and hung up. Unease trickled up his spine. Weird, all right. Maybe it was a janitor or one of Rico's people who did it. It might mean nothing at all.

Then again…it just might.

Candace weighed whether or not to eat another of the cookies her mother had made. It wasn't hunger that drove her to meander around the kitchen and rummage through the cupboards at nine thirty on a rainy November night, but nervous energy. It was too late to call Tracy, and she'd already spoken to her that morning, calling Rick's parents' house in Los Angeles, where Tracy was spending the first part of her Thanksgiving vacation.

"I'm having tons of fun, Mommy," Tracy had assured her. "Nana and I are building a Lego spaceship, and Grandpa is going to teach me how to make applesauce."

Candace had felt a pang then, thinking about Rick wrapped in a Kiss the Cook apron, peeling apples for his family recipe and pretending to be a famous French chef, complete with horrendous imitation accent. She was surprised that the emotion was more happiness than pain, thinking about Tracy carrying forward her father's tradition. They would make the recipe together after she returned, she decided, remembering Rick together with smiles instead of tears.

Thanks, God, Candace thought.

Settling for a glass of water instead of cookies, she carried it to the living room and clicked on the television weather station. The forecaster promised a good drenching, since the incoming storm would intensify in the late evening. Halfway through a round of channel surfing she realized she'd left her cell phone in the bedroom. It wasn't that she expected a call or text, but she felt naked without it, especially since Rico's reign of terror. The moment she stood up to get it, the lights went out.

Fear pricked her spine until she remembered the storm. Electrical outages were not uncommon in Coronado, a peninsula that poked out into the San Diego Bay. Where was the flashlight? "Another good reason not to forget your cell phone," she grumbled to herself.

Figuring she had a better chance of not stubbing her toe going for the kitchen flashlight than her cell phone in the bedroom, she headed there, then rummaged through the messy drawer until she found it. The beam was pretty weak, indicating the batteries were old. Marco would have mumbled something about taking care of safety equipment. The thought brought a smile to her face.

Being in the kitchen also made her remember the grenade that had come sailing through the window. If it hadn't been for Marco… She shivered and rechecked the locks on the kitchen door and the windows. All securely fastened, as she'd known they would be.

Blowing out a breath and determined not to succumb to paranoia, she headed to the bedroom, figuring she could at least entertain herself with her phone until the lights came back on. After padding down the hallway, she pushed open the bedroom door—shocked by the moisture that hit her as soon as she stepped inside.

Droplets of rain splattered through the open window. The window she had left closed and locked. Terror formed slowly, trickling through her senses until her nerves fired to life.

She turned to run, but the bedroom door slammed shut and a palm crushed her lips. She tried to scratch and bite, but her assailant twisted her arms behind her back, then sealed her mouth with a piece of duct tape. Kicking wildly, she knocked over the standing lamp, but couldn't shake off his grip. Her captor shoved her, tumbling, onto the carpet. His weight pinned her down as he flipped her on her stomach and looped tape around her wrists.

"Let me go!" she silently screamed, but lay helpless, trapped, fear tasting like bile in her mouth.

The pressure of his knees suddenly went away and she was hoisted to her feet and tossed onto the bed. She scuttled backward, her body thrumming with terror, until her spine rammed against the headboard and there was nowhere else to go.

Her attacker sat in a chair and flicked a flashlight to life.

Her eyes slowly adjusted.

Jay Rico settled gingerly back onto the cushion. "Hello, baby," he said. "Did you miss me? We've got some unfinished business."

TWENTY

Marco clicked the wipers onto High, rain slicking the windshield as he drove slowly by Candace's cottage after picking up his truck from repair shop. The vehicle still needed a paint job, but that would have to wait. All was quiet and still in the watery moonlight. Of course it was. What had he expected? With each moment, he became more convinced that he was losing his mind, falling prey to loneliness or sentimentality or some such drivel.

Lon and Dan had done some poking around at Marco's request, and there had been no reports of any victims fitting Rico's description, with multiple gunshot wounds to the chest, admitted into local hospitals. The Pack leader had not surfaced anywhere. Further, Lon informed him, rumor on the street was that the Pack was now being led by a guy nicknamed Big Dog, who Marco recognized from his initial research as one of Rico's henchmen. Tensions and violence had escalated between the rival clans, two bullies out to seize control of the block. Not his problem.

But something in his gut, something way down deep, would simply not be calmed since he'd heard about Rico's cleaned-out locker.

Marco was operating under a self-imposed reconnaissance-only mandate. Under no circumstances did he intend to admit his nighttime protection detail to the Gallaghers. It would embarrass him to no end if Candace knew he was again docked in the marina, and had been stationed in his truck a block from her house for the past two nights. *Just until they find Rico's body*, he told himself. *Then I'll disappear again, and no one needs to be the wiser.*

In the daytime, he was careful to keep out of sight and even catch the occasional nap. It wasn't as if he needed regular sleep, anyway. During the most rigorous period of his Basic Underwater Demolitions SEAL training, he'd survived on four hours of sleep for the entire week. After that, any sustained slumber seemed luxurious.

Bear didn't mind the sleeping arrangements as long as he got an outing to the beach during the day, time to explore the dog park when Candace was safely at work, and the opportunity to gnaw on the bones Marco purchased for him. Now he lay in the passenger seat, his front legs dangling over the edge.

"You'd be more comfortable in the backseat, you know," Marco said to him.

The dog opened one eye as if to say *Yeah, right, like that's going to happen.* Marco couldn't blame him. He never wanted to be relegated to the rear seat, either. Was he now imagining threats where there were none, to insert himself back into some dreamed-up mission? A manufactured way to get back into the driver's seat?

He squirmed, fingering the keys in the ignition. If he slunk away, no one would ever know.

Just like the past two nights, the street was quiet. Rain glazed the pavement. No lights showed inside her cottage; they'd flicked off a few moments after he'd arrived on watch, probably as Candace made her way to the back of the house. No porch light was on. He shook his head. How many times had he advised her to leave a light on at night, or at least get a sensor to turn the thing on automatically if anyone approached? Basic safety 101.

"It's on my to-do list," she'd told him time after time. He'd have installed the thing himself, but that would have probably been too pushy, he supposed.

He made the turn around the corner so he could see the back of the house over the fence. Still no lights on. Unusual. He took the night vision binoculars from the glove box. The backyard looked secure, if dark.

"You're paranoid," he muttered aloud. "She's gone to bed, that's all." Bear cracked an eye again to see if his master was showing any signs of exiting the car, or just talking to himself, as was becoming a habit.

Marco was about to put the binoculars away when he thought he caught a sound of breaking glass. Immediately, he put the binoculars to his eyes again. Still nothing out of the ordinary, but no lights, either. He strained to hear. Had it been the rain? His own imagination?

Looking closer, he saw the bedroom window was open. His nerves sprang to life.

Could she have forgotten to close it before the rain started?

Trust your instincts, Quidel.

His instincts told him it was time to swallow his pride and stop hiding in the shadows. If he was wrong, he'd be mortified, and Candace would be furious. If he was right...

Noiselessly, he got out of the truck and told Bear to fall in behind.

Candace stared at Rico, breathing hard over the top of the duct tape. She shouldn't have been completely surprised. Marco had been adamant about his concern that Rico's body hadn't been located. *Right again, Marco.* Still, she found herself in a state of shock at the sight of him. Rico looked thin, his face haggard and his movements slow and stiff, as if he was in pain.

"Didn't think I survived the shooting?" He laughed, then winced and pressed a hand to his ribs. "I've been through worse than that. The irony is, the day of the shooting I was thinking of "going slick" as your navy SEAL would say, and leaving my body armor at home. But at the last minute I put it on. Saved my life, though I got plenty of broken ribs as a souvenir. Been lying low, letting things settle out." He smiled. "How about you, baby? Enjoying things now that you're back in your own digs?"

She forced herself to breathe slower through her nose, though every muscle was taut with fear.

"Don't have anything to say?" He laughed. "That's okay. I don't like chatty women, anyway." He leaned back in the chair and put one booted foot up on the bed as if they were two old friends, catching up.

Her mind raced. What could she do to attract attention, or buy time? Distract him? How, when she was trussed and gagged? Her helplessness nearly choked her. *Keep your head, Candace.*

"I can see that you're confused about why I'm here," he said. "After all, we'd concluded our business, hadn't we? The trial was called off and all. Kevin Tooley, aka Fuzz, is a free man and we've got no beef anymore, right? So why am I here? you're probably wondering. I mean, it was plenty of trouble to knock out the power and climb in through the window, especially with banged-up ribs."

Her cell phone rang on the bedside table. *Let me answer it*, she tried to say. To her amazement he reached toward the phone. Was he going to get it? If it was any of her sisters, they'd alert the police as soon as he got out a single word. Or maybe he would let her answer and she could somehow communicate her desperate situation.

"Did you want to answer this?" he said, smiling. He picked up the phone and checked the caller ID. "Oh, look at that. It's from Popeye, your sailor man."

Marco! Her heart leaped until she considered that he was probably calling from Mexico. Still, he would move mountains to get her help if she could only somehow let him know. She leaned toward the phone.

"That's nice of him to call and check on you, huh?" Rico's eyes glittered. "You sure would like to talk to him, wouldn't you?"

Her breath was coming in panicked bursts now, but she tried not to show it. She pictured Marco there on the other end of the line as the rings sounded one after the other. Grinning widely, Rico held the phone to her lips and put his finger on the answer call button, another on the edge of the duct tape.

"What am I thinking?" he said suddenly, sitting back. "You're all tied up at the moment." He pulled the phone away, pressed a few buttons, nodded once and tossed it into the garbage can, chuckling as her stomach plummeted.

"Too bad. Popeye's gonna have to leave a voice mail, 'cuz we still got business. Know why? Fuzz has gone over to the dark side now, joined up with the Cliffs, and he thinks his father is a scumbag." Jay's eyes locked on to hers. "Know who caused that to happen?"

She felt her lungs constrict at the coldness in his eyes.

"You."

The word shot through her like a bullet. In that moment she knew he was going to kill her. The conversation was just for his enjoyment, to prolong the pleasure like a cat toying with a trapped bird, the same way he'd behaved on the fire escape. How could she free herself without even being able to keep him talking? Frantic, she tried wriggling her hands behind her back to loosen the tape.

Rico clucked his tongue as if he was scolding a child. "You told Kevin all about me, didn't you? That I'm his father and that I ran down his mother."

She shook her head.

"I know you talked to the doc at the clinic who treated Yolanda, and you even visited dear old granny's apartment. You did your detective thing and put all the clues together and you told my son. Aren't…you…clever?" He punctuated each word with a kick on the mattress that sent her wobbling.

She felt the headboard to see if there was a sharp bit of wood or screw she might use to saw through the binding. Her pulse revved higher when she felt the end of a nail poking out through the wood. She pressed the tape against it and felt the metal punch through. Slowly she began to ease her wrists up and down in an attempt to widen the hole she'd made, or at least weaken the tape enough that she could snap it. Rico didn't seem to notice.

"I loved Yolanda, and I know I shouldn't have killed her, but she was going to leave me, you know? She didn't want our son anywhere near me. I couldn't stand the thought of her moving on, and maybe giving my son to another man someday, so I lost it." He shook his head. "I wish I hadn't done it, but she shouldn't have pushed me so far. You can't unpour the milk, you know?"

So it was Yolanda Tooley's own fault she'd been murdered? Rico was disgusting, the classic abuser, but with supreme effort Candace kept the disdain from her face.

Rico was looking at her thoughtfully. "Like I told you before, a man has to draw his battle lines, right?"

She nodded to keep him talking, feeling the tear in the tape growing wider. Her hope grew with each millimeter.

Rico groaned and pressed his hand to his side. "All the work I've done to keep that kid safe and now guess what? My own son is gunning for my life. And not just him." Rico's mouth tightened into a hard line. "Word is out that I'm alive, but weak, you know? All the dogs are tracking me, sniffing for my blood, and who's leading the hunt?" He slammed a palm down on the bedside table, making her jump. "My son. My own kid wants me dead. What do you think of that?"

A hot trickle slid down her wrist—blood from where the tape was cutting into her. With a surge of elation, she felt her hands part, but tried not to let her posture give it away. Her wrists were free, but what should her next action be? To run for the door and hope she could make it out to the street before Rico caught her? The little spurt of hope flamed higher in her heart. She'd escaped him before, and she'd do it again with God's help. Slowly, she moved one foot closer to the edge of the bed to give herself leverage.

Rico sat up straighter. "So I'm gonna have to show them, right? The Cliffs? My son? I'm gonna have to let them all know my territory is not for sale. I am not weak." The curtains swayed in the breeze and more rain was propelled in, spattering them both. Rico paid it no heed. "That means no mercy, and anyone who has crossed me will wind up dead.

"Know who is at the top of that list?" He smiled and planted his feet carefully on the floor. She froze as he took a gun from his pocket. "You, baby. You started this whole mess, and you turned my son against me. So now you're gonna die."

After receiving no answer to his call, Marco sprinted along the wet sidewalk and let himself and Bear into the backyard. He raced to the open bedroom window, standing underneath and listening. A man's low voice carried over the rain. Didn't matter what he was saying, Marco knew it was Rico.

There was no time to get Lon or the cops. He was going to have to complete this mission solo. He worked his way around the house, checking doors, which he found to be locked. There was no other quick entrance. The window must be how Rico got in. Marco could force entry, but the noise would alert him, and it might be too late for Candace. Only one way to go, he figured.

"Bear, stay and watch," he commanded.

The dog sat immediately, heedless of the falling

rain, eyes riveted on Marco as he climbed up on the air-conditioning unit and hoisted himself onto the roof. The rain made the tile surface slippery and he had to go slow. He slithered to the position just above Candace's bedroom window. Stress was making his pulse hammer out of control, so he did some tactical breathing to slow the rampaging adrenaline. He had only one chance and he couldn't let nerves get in the way.

Keep talking, Rico, he willed. *You're never going to see me coming.*

He gave himself a slow count to three. Then he gripped the edge of the gutter, swung his body down over the eaves and let his momentum send him hurtling through the bedroom window.

TWENTY-ONE

Candace would have screamed if her mouth wasn't taped. Her brain couldn't quite process what she was witnessing. In a shower of glass, Marco Quidel erupted through the bedroom window. He was on his feet, diving across the room at Rico, before she had time to pull her hands from behind her back,

Rico fired a shot that shattered the mirror above her wardrobe.

"Get out," Marco shouted to her, locked in a battle over Rico's gun. A second shot took a chunk out of the wall behind her. Keeping as low as she could, she ran to the living room, hands trembling wildly as she ripped the tape off her mouth, grabbed the house phone and dialed 911, gasping out her name and address.

"Ma'am," the dispatcher said. "Get out of the house and wait for the police. They're en route as we speak."

"I have to help him," she panted.

"Ma'am, exit the house immediately and wait for an officer."

Every nerve in Candace's body screamed for her to follow the dispatcher's directions and run, but she would not, could not leave Marco. She dropped the phone as the thud of bodies hitting the wall vibrated the floor under her feet. Where could she find a weapon? Her pepper spray was in the bedroom. A knife from the kitchen? She didn't think she could manage to hold on to one, let alone use it. She grabbed the first thing she saw, a wooden chair, and ran back to the bedroom.

Marco had his opponent up against the wall, one hand on Rico's throat and the other pinning his gun hand. Outside, she heard Bear barking ferociously.

"Police are on their way," she panted. "Give it up, Rico."

In spite of Marco's interference, Rico pulled the trigger. The shot arced to the metal window frame, ricocheting and skimming Marco's shoulder. He jerked and tumbled onto his back. Rico broke from his grasp.

She swung the chair as hard as she could, but her aim was off. Rico escaped and Marco rolled aside in time to avoid the flying furniture.

Candace ran for the door, but Marco caught her ankle before she crossed the threshold, causing her to stumble to one knee.

"No," he grunted.

"He's not going to get away," she said, trying to tug free, adrenaline roaring like the surf inside her. "Let me go."

Instead, Marco got to his feet and pushed her behind him. He stopped at the doorway and listened. Grabbing a pillow from her chair, he tossed it into the hall. The shots came immediately, a procession of hot metal that blasted the pillow to pieces.

That would have been me, she thought, her mouth dry.

Sirens wailed and they heard the front door flung open, the sound of running feet as Rico escaped into the night.

Candace let out a groan of frustration.

Marco looked at her, panting. "Hurt?"

"No."

Muttering something she couldn't catch, he returned to the window.

"What are you doing?"

"Gotta calm the dog down before he gets himself shot by the cops." Marco called out the window to quiet Bear and gave him a stern stay command. Then he turned to her, still breathing hard and sweating.

"Police are about to make entry and they're going to be amped, so we're not going to make any sudden moves here, okay?"

That was easy to accomplish, as her legs were shaking so badly she could hardly stand. He picked up the overturned chair and ushered her into it. Then he sat calmly on the bed, hands splayed on the rumpled comforter so the cops could easily see he wasn't armed.

It was the most ridiculous scene she could imagine. Her house had been shot to pieces. Rico the dead gangster was not really dead. And Marco was sitting on the bed looking as composed as if he was waiting for a bus.

How did you know? Why did you come? She wanted to ask, but was distracted by the sight of the blood staining his left shoulder.

"You're hurt."

"Not deep."

"How can you tell?"

"Just can."

And that was all she was likely to get out of him on the topic. "How did you know Rico was coming tonight?"

"I didn't." He quirked a smile.

"What can you possibly be smiling about?"

"Because you brought a chair to a gunfight. I like that, except that you almost clobbered me with it."

A half-hysterical giggle bubbled out. "I guess I did. If I had known you were coming, I would have been more prepared." She looked at him, still not quite believing that Marco Quidel was actually back, sitting quietly on her bed, bleeding from a shoulder wound he'd incurred while saving her life, and teasing her. "Marco, what in the world are you doing here?"

"Tell you in a minute. Stay still. Here they come." The floor shuddered and the room was filled with noise and activity as four police officers, guns drawn, burst into the room.

* * *

They assembled at the PCI office at just after midnight. Dr. Dan cleaned and taped up Marco's shoulder and didn't even bother to suggest that he should visit a hospital. Marco had to admit the guy was a good doctor. Donna, Angela and JeanBeth made sure he and Candace were sufficiently warm, hydrated and generally fussed over.

Lon arrived and took his customary place slouched against the wall.

"Police are going to investigate, but since there's no trial, there's no offer of police protection," Donna said. "So I think we're pretty much on our own this time."

JeanBeth frowned. "Their priorities are on the escalating gang conflict. Rico is somewhat of a rogue right now. He's got some loyal Pack followers, but others have split off to follow this man named Big Dog. It's a turf war."

"That works to our advantage, because he has to watch his back," Marco said. "He doesn't have his army behind him and he's distracted."

"Not that distracted," Candace said. "He made it clear he blames me for turning Kevin against him, and he won't stop until I'm dead."

She sounded calm when she said it, but Marco could read the underlying tension. Still, she was keeping it together, and she was more determined than any of them to bring Rico to justice. He got an image of her hurling the chair and suppressed a smile. "Tracy is safest staying with her grandparents right now," he said. Then he amended, "That is my opinion, I meant. Do we agree on that?"

There were nods all around.

"Back to the beach house?" Angela said.

"Yes. All of us, I would suggest," Marco said.

Candace fiddled with her mug of tea. "To sit and wait again? For how long? Forever?"

"No," Marco said.

"Why? How is this different?" she demanded.

"Because this time we're playing offense."

"What do you mean?" JeanBeth said. "How?"

"Remember Rico's guy Champ? The one with the missing tooth? I've heard he's still in the area, and he knows all of Rico's hiding places. He's gonna help us find him."

"What if he's not cooperative? He gave us up at the clinic."

"Maybe not. It's possible he was really there to stop things. Either way, he knows Rico and he knows his habits. If there's any way to get to him, Champ's our best resource."

"How do we find him?" Donna demanded.

Dan took out his cell phone and slid it across the table to Marco. "His last known address is on the screen."

Marco couldn't hide his surprise.

Dan shrugged. "I figured if you were going off on your own to capture Rico, I might as well see if I could dig up some info to help you. He's a local boy, and I didn't figure gang life would provide health coverage, so I checked at all the free clinics in the Long Beach and Los Angeles areas where I had some friends working. Champ had gone to one for stitches so..." He shrugged. "I called in a favor."

Angela's look of shock changed to wonderment, and she threw her arms around his neck and kissed him.

Marco allowed a smile. "You're all right, Doc."

"Just trying to keep up with all these private eye and Navy SEAL types."

Marco looked at Lon. "This would be easier if Dev were here, too, but we'll have to make it work. You got time tomorrow to go with me and lean on Champ?"

Lon gave one short nod.

"We all have time to help," JeanBeth said.

He didn't argue. "All right. Make your way up to the Party Palace, but not all at once. I don't think Rico's got good surveillance help, since he's on his own and Baxter isn't feeding him information, but we'll take care, anyway. We'll work it through tomorrow."

Marco approached Candace. "Ready to go?"

She sighed. "This all feels so terribly familiar."

"This time it's going to be different."

"Does this mean you're returning to PCI?" she asked.

"Temporarily."

She didn't ask anything further until they were in the truck and rolling toward Long Beach.

"So Marco, why did you decide to come back?"

"Lots of little things were bugging me. I guess we should just chalk it up to instinct."

"You've been watching my house, haven't you?"

He shot her a sidelong glance. "How much trouble am I going to be in if I say yes?"

She sighed. "I guess not much, since you saved me from Rico." A mischievous grin lit her face. "Are you sure your nickname isn't Secret Agent Man?"

He laughed. "Yes, I'm sure, and don't ask because I'm not telling."

"Okay." She leaned her head against the headrest and closed her eyes. "I thought maybe you came back because you missed me."

More like ached for you. He shut down the thought. *This is going to end soon and Rico will lose and I will leave.* It was the right choice for Candace and Tracy. They deserved a happy future, so he'd give it to them, but first he had to deal with one last, very dangerous obstacle.

Coming for you, Jay Rico.

TWENTY-TWO

The information from Dan's contact indicated that Champ lived most recently in a trailer at a nearby RV park. It was agreed that Angela and Candace would check in at the desk and try to sweet-talk some information out of the clerk. Working in teams, the investigators would put a tail on Champ and corner him when he left the park, so as not to force a dangerous confrontation close to any residents. With the plan as firm as possible, they headed out. The drive took them an hour, the two sisters in Angela's car, Marco and Lon in the truck, and Dan, Donna and Jean-Beth in another vehicle, planning to take up position at the trailer park's back exit in case Champ should become aware of their presence too soon and attempt to bolt. They would have an excellent view of the comings and goings.

The clerk was a friendly woman with a puff of white hair and a plaid dress. She was eager to talk about anything and everything. Angela finally maneuvered the conversation to the subject of Champ.

"Oh, sure. Champ's a quiet fellow. Don't have a phone number for him or anything. He keeps to himself, but I can leave a message for him under his mat. That's what we usually do for our residents." She gave them a slightly disapproving look. "I can't tell you which one's his place, of course, because that would be giving out private information."

"We understand," Candace said. "If you could just give him this message, he can call me." She scrawled a made-up number on a pad that the clerk offered. "Thanks so much."

"Glad to help," she said. "Champ could use some visitors."

Angela and Candace left, waving to the clerk as they drove out of the park.

JeanBeth radioed in less than five minutes. "She's putting the note on the end unit, white trailer with blue trim."

"Hooray for binoculars and Mom's eagle eyes," Angela said.

They watched for the better part of the day from a discreet distance, but no one came or went from Champ's trailer. Candace's back was aching from sitting. "Whoever said detective work was glamorous never did any of it."

"He might have gotten wind of what happened at your cottage last night with Rico, and taken off."

Candace groaned at the prospect of another dead end.

Angela grabbed her arm. "Look. There he is. He's heading for his car."

Champ got into a tan two-door and drove out the front entrance. Angela and Candace ducked down as he passed, and then followed along behind. When he left the graveled drive and turned onto the main road, the traffic became heavier. Angela and Candace struggled to keep him in view for the next few miles amid the bustling traffic.

"I lost him," Angela said. "Where did he go?"

Candace strained at the seat belt. "There." She pointed. He'd turned into a small parking lot that faced a strip mall. There was a tiny grocery, a comic book store, and a gas station on the corner. Champ headed into the grocery shop. Marco and Lon pulled up in the parking space on the driver's side of his car. Dan made Donna and JeanBeth join the other women in their vehicle before he pulled in on the passenger side.

Donna flopped into the backseat with her mother and slammed the door in a huff. "Your fiancé is bossy, Angela."

Angela laughed. "Then he fits well in this family. He's

trying to protect you and Mom. Brent would totally concur and you know it."

She grumbled something. "Anyway, he said to keep back a couple of yards and follow him if he takes off."

They waited a painful ten minutes before Champ reappeared with a paper sack of groceries and a newspaper tucked under his arm.

Oblivious, he fished for his keys, before he noticed Marco leaning on his driver's side door. He stiffened, eyes darting to the passenger side, where Lon stood, palms drumming on the roof of Champ's car.

"Is he going to run?" JeanBeth whispered.

Candace gripped the door handle, ready to chase him on foot if that's what it took.

Angela inched the car closer, near enough that Champ realized he would not be able to back out of the space, either. She lowered the window so they could hear the conversation, but kept the engine running. Candace moved to get out of the car, but Angela shook her head.

Teeth clenched, Candace listened in.

Champ squeezed the bag against his side. "I don't want trouble."

"Neither do we," Marco said. "We want Jay Rico."

"He's dead."

"No, he's not, so quit giving us the runaround."

"Don't ask me. I'm out of the Pack, what's left of it," Champ said.

"Yeah? Then you can give us some info. You're not a fan of Rico's. You were ready to turn on him at the clinic, or so you said. Was that just a lie you spewed out when I caught you in the stairwell?"

"Nah. Rico was acting more and more crazy, taking wild risks to get Fuzz out of jail. Showing up at a clinic? Man! Suicide. Couple of us figured we'd wave you and the girl off before Rico got there, but we were too late."

"Why did you want to help us?"

"I didn't," Champ snarled. "I wanted to keep Rico from losing it. Didn't want him shooting up the clinic and getting us all arrested." He blew out a breath. "I did everything for him. I was faithful, paid my dues, and got nothing to show for it. Plus some of us were wondering why he fawned over Fuzz. Now I find out he kept it secret about Fuzz being his son. That wasn't cool, man. It was like lying to all of us. Never lifted a finger to keep my brother out of prison and expected us all to take crazy risks for his own kid."

"So you're gonna help us?" Marco said.

Champ looked from him to Lon. "No, I'm not."

Candace's spirits plummeted. He was too scared of Rico. In a way she didn't blame him.

Marco cocked his head, considering. If he was disappointed with Champ's decision not to assist, he didn't show it.

"Actually, I think you are going to help us," he said.

"Why would I do that?"

"Because deep down you're worried that when Rico takes control of the Pack again, he's going to start by cleaning house. He'll reward those that stood by him and punish the ones who didn't. That's you, Champ. He won't forgive and he won't forget, not ever."

Champ scuffed his toe in the dirt.

"All you need to do," Marco said, "is tell me how to get him."

"You tried, and the Cliffs, too. He's still alive and a free man. Untouchable."

"Not this time. He shot up Candace's house, so the cops can make an arrest if we find him. Are any of his chop shops still in operation? Or maybe you have an idea about where he's holing up."

Champ grimaced, but Candace's heartbeat ticked up at

the tell on his face. He knew, or he suspected where Rico might be, she was sure of it.

Marco stared at him. "Give me an address and we'll drive away, business over, and never bother you again."

Champ looked again from Marco to Lon. "You don't know who you're messing with."

Marco's expression turned to hard steel. "Yes, we do."

"If you don't get him quick, he'll kill you."

"He's not going to get the chance," Marco said. "We'll find him, bring in the cops, and he's out of the picture."

Candace felt again the sensation of being bound and gagged, Rico fueling her terror word by word before he tried to shoot her in her own home, in Tracy's home. What if Tracy had been there instead of visiting her grandparents? Candace shut down the thought and whispered to her sister, "What if he doesn't cooperate?"

Angela shook her head. "We'll have to find another way."

But there was no other way and they both knew it. The seconds ticked by. If Champ insisted on leaving, there would be little they could do to stop him. She clenched her hands and prayed that he would cooperate.

"Okay," he said finally.

Candace felt like shouting in exultation out the window, but she didn't want to miss a word.

"I know where one of his shops is. It's still operating, and Rico hangs there sometimes."

"Address?" Marco asked.

"Outside of Brewster, on Rich Street in a warehouse. I heard they got an overload of product, and Rico's gonna be there tonight to collect his money." Champ glared at him. "Now can I go?"

Marco moved aside and the man got into the car.

"Remember what I said," Champ said out his open window.

Candace knew every syllable. *If you don't get him quick, he'll kill you.*

Angela moved her car and Marco and Lon watched Champ drive away. Dan got out and joined them. "So you got what you needed?" he asked.

Marco nodded.

"What?" Candace said, noting the hesitation in his eyes. "Something is bothering you."

Marco stared in the direction Champ had taken. "He may have just handed us the key to getting Rico once and for all."

Candace waited for the rest.

"But he also might be laying a trap to get into Rico's good graces again."

"How will we know which one it is?"

It was Lon who finally spoke up. "When the bullets start flying."

That evening they were in position, in the town of Brewster, with much the same setup as the first time they'd tried to bust Rico's chop shop. Now it was Marco and Lon who were ready to make entry into the warehouse. Candace and her sisters were relieved to see both men wearing body armor. This time, both were also armed with guns, she knew.

"What about the police?" she'd said again, just before they had made the drive to Brewster.

"We'll confirm that he's there, and we'll call them in. If we tell them beforehand they'll try to make a bust and scare him off," Marco said.

She had shoved down the worries that threatened to claw their way to the surface. How could they be in the same frightening situation as that first time, when Dev had been injured?

"So that means you're going to be careful," she said, touching her fingers to his cheek. His skin was roughened with a five o'clock shadow that tickled and made her want to stroke the hard edge of his jaw. *A good man*, her heart told her. She was deeply grateful in that moment that the Lord had put Marco into her life.

"Always." His gaze met hers and then flicked away, as if the connection caused him pain.

I'm sorry, Marco. I'm sorry I can't be what you need, what you deserve.

Outside the warehouse, JeanBeth switched on Lon's camera. "Now listen to me," she said to the men. "I will have no one getting hurt on this mission. Am I making myself clear?"

"Yes, ma'am," both answered.

"Okay then," she said, kissing them each on the cheek before they crossed the darkened street.

Candace didn't think her heart could accelerate much faster, but it was pounding away in her chest like a runaway horse. The laptop feed showed Marco and Lon approaching, making their way around the side to the back. With each step she thought about Champ. He might have laid a perfect trap. And how would they know?

When the bullets start flying.

Candace's mother gripped her shoulder, Angela took her hand and together they poured out prayers for the safety of the two men.

Lon's camera showed Marco testing the door. It swung open under his fingertips, unlocked. Candace's body tensed as they entered, as if she, too, were creeping along with them into the darkness.

The space was crowded with car parts, pallets and an entire vehicle up on jacks, clear evidence that a chop shop was operating there. She sat up straighter. The cops could arrest Rico this time.

The door in the back must lead to the room Champ had described, the office and Rico's home away from home.

Marco and Lon approached, and JeanBeth held the cell phone, ready to alert the police.

"Just one look and get out," Candace whispered, though they couldn't hear her.

Marco and Lon stopped and froze, listening, Candace imagined. Had they heard something? The tension was unbearable.

There was a small window above the door. Marco knelt and Lon used Marco's bent leg for a boost to climb up. The camera panned across the wood, dizzying her until Lon reached the top.

"What's in there? Can you see?" Candace muttered.

Slowly, Lon's camera picked up the view inside.

With her breath held prisoner in her lungs, she strained forward as the seconds ticked on.

TWENTY-THREE

Lon jumped down and Marco knew it was all over.

"Nothing," Lon said. "No one there."

Marco slapped his thigh in disgust and used the radio. "Got anything out there?"

"All quiet," Dan responded.

He was glad it wasn't Candace who answered. He didn't want to hear the disappointment in her voice as she realized they'd been thwarted again.

"You figure Champ warned him off?" Lon said.

"Looks that way, but they didn't have time to clean it out properly this time."

They checked again for any hidden dangers and found nothing, nor did they find anything that might indicate where Rico could be.

"I'm coming in," Candace said over the radio.

Lon raised an eyebrow. "Gonna try to talk Gumdrop out of it?"

"Wouldn't do any good, anyway."

She came in with Angela and JeanBeth behind her.

"Dan and Donna are keeping watch," Angela said. "So far there's nothing. He said he'll call the cops in fifteen minutes to report a suspected chop shop at this address."

"There must be something here that can tell us where he is," Candace insisted.

Lon put his hand on the office door.

"Easy," Marco said. His suspicion was born of long hot days in deserts and jungles where the threats were unending and unexpected.

Lon nudged the door open a fraction. “Looks clear.”

Marco handed him a flashlight. “Look again.”

Lon shone the flashlight into the crack, then peered closer. He straightened with a sheepish grin. “Sorry, Chief. You were right.”

“What is it?” JeanBeth asked.

“Trip wire,” Lon said. He took a knife from his belt and disconnected the wire before he slowly opened the door.

Marco and Lon went first. It was a crude device. Stepping into the wire would have triggered the mechanism to detonate rounds of ammo. Lon set the thing on the floor with gloved hands. It might give the cops something to work with.

Candace stepped into the room, ignoring Marco’s objections.

“He couldn’t have had enough time to remove everything.” She went to a small bed in the corner with a sleeping bag tossed over it. On the floor was a pair of balled up socks and a gym bag with running shoes and a half-empty water bottle. “Maybe it’s enough for the police to prove he was here along with these stolen cars.”

Marco didn’t answer. He had his doubts about the police being able to do anything to Jay Rico.

A phone rang, the sound loud in the dusty warehouse. Marco shot a look of disapproval at the women. “Didn’t remember to silence your phones?”

“That’s not mine,” JeanBeth said. “I’m not a complete amateur, you know.”

Candace went to the corner and pulled her jacket over her hand before she picked something up. “It’s here, a cell phone,” she said. “It’s got to be him calling.”

The phone rang again. Marco moved to take it from her, but she’d already answered, holding it to her ear.

Fifteen seconds ticked by, but that quarter of a minute visibly changed Candace Gallagher. Terror erased the life and spirit from her expression, the color completely drained from her cheeks and she staggered as if Jay Rico had walked into the room and struck her.

Marco leaped forward and grabbed the phone, jamming it to his ear in time to hear Rico's soft laughter before the dial tone. Enraged, he threw it down. How could he keep losing to this guy?

JeanBeth reached Candace first. "What it is, honey?" she said.

"Rico," she whispered.

Her mother gripped her hand. "What did he say?"

She opened her mouth to talk, then swallowed convulsively. "Three rings," she said.

Marco wondered if there had been something more, but that was enough, wasn't it? Rico intended to follow through, terrorizing her until the final ring.

"He's not gonna win, Candace," Marco said.

But she didn't seem to hear. Her eyes were fixed on some faraway spot where he couldn't reach her, like the place where Gwen had been when he'd lost her, too.

No. He wouldn't allow it.

"Cops are on their way," Dan said over the radio. "Coming out?"

Candace was being guided to the door by JeanBeth and Angela. JeanBeth shot a worried look over Candace's shoulder, a look that said *There's got to be a way out of this.*

There was, and he was going to find it.

They drove back to the beach house and Dan threw down a sleeping bag on the floor to bunk with Marco and Lon. The house gradually subsided into silence. Marco couldn't sleep. Instead he paced in maddening circles around the family room. Finally, he sank into a chair and looked at the mess from every angle. He was putting together yet another possible scenario for how he would capture Rico when he heard the sound of someone easing slowly down the stairs.

Candace tiptoed toward the front door, fully clothed, wearing a jacket and his black baseball cap pulled low over her hair. She didn't see him in the shadows and for a moment he was too startled to speak.

She slowly turned the handle and opened the door, stepping outside.

At one o'clock in the morning?

The cool night air embraced him as he followed her onto the porch. "Where are you going?"

She yelped and turned. Her face was stark white in the moonlight. "Nowhere. Go back to sleep."

"I wasn't asleep, and you're not out for a moonlit stroll, so what's going on?"

He wished he could read the expression on her face. All he could see was the frown and her eyes glimmering like the deepest ocean water.

She exhaled, her breath slow and shaky. "I know you don't want to hear this, but I'm leaving for a couple of hours and I'm not going to tell you where I'm going."

He folded his arms across his chest. "Okay. Then I'll come with you until I find out for myself."

"No," she said. "I don't want you to."

"Under the present circumstances, it doesn't matter."

"Yes, it does," she snapped.

He shook his head. "I go with you or I follow behind. Your choice."

She pushed back the hair spilling from under the cap. "I don't want you with me, Marco. Can't you understand? I don't want you here, or in my life or Tracy's." The last syllable came out as a sob.

He swallowed. "I know that. I… I will leave after this is sorted out, like I said."

Misery shone in her eyes even in the darkness. "I'm sorry, but it's got to be now. I can't have you around, not for one more minute."

The words cleaved a trail of pain in his heart. *Don't want you here. Can't have you around.* "When Rico's caught—"

"No," she snapped. "We've been tiptoeing around things long enough. I can't love another man. I won't." Tears sparkled on her lashes. "I'm sorry, I really am."

He gazed at her and the pain of what she'd said was nearly unbearable, because he knew it was the truth. She didn't want him, not in the way he desperately desired. So be it. Through the hurt that throbbed inside him, he couldn't silence the suspicion that something was wrong, very, very wrong. He waited for her next move.

"I'm going and I don't want you to follow me."

"I see."

"Promise."

"I will promise," he said slowly, "and I'll get in my truck and drive away right now and never come back, if you tell me one thing."

She paused. "What?"

"What did Rico really say in that phone call?"

Silence. One second, two, five.

"I..." she whispered.

"You have to tell me."

She began to tremble all over, and then she slid to her knees. He caught her before she made it fully to the ground. Sobs wrenched out of her, the sound of sorrow so profound it stripped his breath away.

"What it is, Candace?"

"Rico has Tracy," she gasped, before she slumped into his arms.

She felt herself being carried back inside and placed on the sofa. Her body betrayed her, lungs panting wildly, but unable to supply enough oxygen. Her head spun and her vision began to narrow. Marco knelt at her knees, forcing her to look at him.

"I want you to breathe with me for a minute. Breathe in and hold it, then out. We're gonna do that a couple of times, okay?" He held her chilled hands and she did as he told her until gradually, her lungs seemed to come back to working order.

She squeezed out the words. "Tracy was at her grandparents' in San Diego, but he sent his people there to get her. He told me…he said he would kill her if I didn't come to him tomorrow at the gym."

"Another bluff?"

"No," she said, fighting against a sob. "Rico put Tracy on the phone…she said 'Mommy.'" Agony seared through her, a pain she hadn't felt since the moment the marines knocked on her door to tell her about Rick. The fierce clasp of Marco's hand was the only thing keeping her from falling to the floor.

"Take another breath and tell me the rest."

She pulled in a shuddering gulp of air and tried to expel it slowly. "I called her grandparents. They said last night two men ran them off the road and took her. They were told if they contacted the police…" Hysteria nearly took her down again. "…Tracy would be killed. They were going to call the police, anyway, but they wanted to contact me first. They'd been texting, but I didn't have my phone on."

"So you were going to deliver yourself to Rico? Just like that? Without telling me?"

"He said to come alone, with no cops, or he would kill her." She felt her breathing begin to accelerate again until he tightened his grip on her hands.

"This is a setup to make it easier for him to kill you."

"What choice do I have, Marco?" Tears splashed down onto the front of her jacket. "He's got my baby, and if he sees cops or you or anyone, he'll kill her." Her voice broke. "That monster has my child."

Marco looked at the bag. "What were you planning to do?"

"I don't know. I… I took Lon's gun. Daddy taught me how to shoot." That was the extent of her plan, the only thing her desperate mind could put together. "I have to go, Marco, alone."

He cupped her chin in his hand and the copper fire in his eyes stilled her for a moment. "No. We're going to get her back together."

Together. How she wanted to hold on to that word. Together…she almost believed they could succeed.

"I'm so scared, Marco. I've never been so afraid in my life."

"For God hath not given us the spirit of fear," Marco began.

"But of power, and of love, and of a sound mind," JeanBeth finished. She was standing in the doorway with Angela's arm tight around her. They both looked as scared as Candace felt, but in their faces she saw courage. *And that's what courage is*, she thought suddenly. It wasn't denying the fear or refusing to acknowledge the thing that made your soul quake with fright, it was hanging on to God and trusting Him to walk you through.

She looked at Marco. If he believed they would rescue Tracy, then she could too.

"Power, love and a sound mind," he repeated. "We're going to get her back safe and the good guys are going to win."

"What did I miss?" asked Lon, yawning from the doorway.

She expected Marco to get to his feet and begin making battle plans. Instead, he gestured for JeanBeth and Angela and Lon to come closer. Holding a hand to Candace and reaching for each other, the four of them circled her in prayer.

Mommy's coming, baby.

TWENTY-FOUR

Rico's meeting place was the same gym near where Candace had arranged to talk to him at the deli. At 4:00 a.m. the sun had not yet begun to rise, which worked well for Marco. God had paved the way for him to recruit some help and they were as ready as they were going to get.

In the alley two buildings over, where they'd staged themselves, he checked Candace's body armor one more time.

Lon jogged up. "Tracy's in the back room, upper west corner."

Candace gulped. "How do you know? Is she all right?"

"Thermal scope," Marco said, keeping his eyes on Lon. "Where's Rico?"

"There are two people in front near the boxing ring, one upstairs. Might be more."

"Okay. We've got twenty minutes from my mark before Dan and the others call the cops." He looked at Candace one more time and put his hands on her shoulders, felt her trembling. "We'll get her out, and you wait here for the cops."

"If Rico kills you..." she started, tears rolling down her face.

He sighed and quirked a comic expression. "Then I guess you'll never know my nickname."

She threw her arms around him and the emotion rolled through in a tidal wave that made his skin prickle. "I don't want you to do this," she cried into his shoulder. "You shouldn't be taking this risk. Rico wants *me*."

"He's not going to get what he wants. You have to stay safe. Tracy is going to need her mama."

"She needs her uncle, too," Candace said.

Sweet words, born out of fear and a desperate need, but they didn't echo as loudly as the ones she'd said before. *I don't want you here, or in my life or Tracy's.*

She put her hands on his vest, tracing the front pockets with her palms. "You're too skinny. Where's your body armor?"

The vest he was wearing had pockets for the ballistic plates, but there was no time for him to get them from the *Semper Fortis*. He wanted her to wear Lon's extra set, so he was "going slick," which would enhance his speed, unless, of course, he got shot. He gently moved her away. "Gotta go. Get into the car, stay put and listen in on the radio."

Candace looked at him for what seemed like an eternity and he tried to memorize every detail, her graceful silhouette, the way the breeze caught her hair, her arms wrapped tight around herself as if she was already holding Tracy.

Remember this moment, Marco. How honored he was to be the one to finish the mission, the most important one of his life. He hoped Rick would have trusted him to do the job of saving his family.

Dan, Angela and JeanBeth waited by the car. JeanBeth looked at him and put her hands on her heart, a gesture he understood.

Love you, too, Gallaghers.

Then he detached himself from the emotion, focused on the goal and started to climb up the fire escape ladder. The buildings were close together, so it would be only a three-foot crossing from one to the other using the ropes he had already put in place, and then he'd be on the roof of the gym. Lon had used bolt cutters to gain entry via the padlocked door. They were set and ready to engage the enemy. He allowed a quick look down.

Below him, the Gallaghers and Dan grew smaller and smaller, but he could feel their prayers, their love, the weight of their desperate hopes resting on his shoulders. "I will not fail," he silently promised them.

"Going to bring your girls home safe, Rick," he said silently.

It was go time.

Candace clutched the radio, sandwiched in the backseat between her mother and Angela. Her feet rested on Dan's baseball bat and glove.

"Sorry for the gear," he said. "I didn't take the time to clear out the car after Marco called."

Dan drummed his fingers on the steering wheel until it nearly drove her mad. They listened to the radio check. Candace was startled when she heard a third voice chime in.

"Gumdrop and company still secure, Chief."

"Was that Dev?" she said, incredulous.

Dan smiled. "Yeah. Marco told me his team had returned to the Coronado base due to some technical difficulties with their chopper. Somehow Dev managed to make it back here."

Candace felt a surge of gratitude that these men would put their lives on the line for her daughter. How could anyone repay that debt? she wondered. *By living the life God gave you* was the answer that materialized without warning in her heart.

Living the life God gave her. Did that mean allowing herself to love the man God had placed in her life after her husband? She wasn't sure. What would Rick think about Marco? There was only one answer to that question. He would have deep respect for him, a sense of gratitude and—she shocked herself with the thought—he would find such a man was worthy. Worthy to be a friend, uncle, perhaps even a partner to Candace?

The radio crackled, disturbing her thoughts.

"One hostile down," Lon said, his voice barely audible.

Her throat clogged. "Does that mean they found her?" Her fingers dug into the upholstery. *Tracy*, her heart screamed. What if Rico had hurt her? Or worse? Was this all a ruse and they would be too late to rescue her daughter? It would be like Rico to torture her by taking her child, like he believed she'd done to him.

Her ears buzzed and her vision began to grow fuzzy as she struggled to keep her breathing in rhythm. *I will not give in to the spirit of fear.* Her mother nearly crushed her hand in a ferocious grasp.

"Do they have Tracy?" Candace whispered. "Please let them have her."

No one answered and the minutes marched on with agonizing slowness. If they really had found Tracy, Lon would be bringing her down the back staircase. Marco would provide cover for the escape and then the cops would be summoned. But there were so many variables that could result in disaster, dozens of ways the mission could go disastrously wrong.

The relentless silence continued. Candace's body was bathed in cold sweat. Try as she might, her lungs wouldn't take in enough air. Her cell phone rang and she answered.

"Two rings, baby," Rico said. "Better be on your way before the last ring."

He clicked off and she clutched the phone, sucking in breath to keep from screaming.

"Two rings," she whispered. JeanBeth murmured prayer after prayer, still clutching her hands, and Angela held her from the other side.

Why would no one speak over the radio? It was a trap. Rico had killed Marco and Tracy. He was a madman and he'd won. Panic overwhelmed Candace's senses. She pushed at her sister. "I have to get out."

Angela held her in place against her struggles. "You can't.

"Let me go," she sobbed. "I have to get to her. He's going to kill Marco and my baby."

"Candace!" Angela said, fighting to keep her in place.

Candace felt a scream working its way up her throat when a figure appeared at the end of the alley. She froze.

Who was it? One of Rico's guys?

She feared she was going to faint. Faster and faster the black blur approached, as Dan started the car and put it in Reverse, ready to escape.

The runner grew close enough for Candace to recognize. She screamed and threw herself from the car after Angela as Lon put Tracy down.

"Mommy?" she said tentatively, one hand over her eyes to shield them from the headlights.

Candace couldn't get any words out through her clogged throat and the tears that blinded her. She stumbled toward her daughter, falling to one knee and catching her up in a wild embrace. Her daughter, her child, back in her arms. Her heart cried out to God for His bottomless mercy.

Angela and JeanBeth drew close, Dan a pace behind.

"L-Lon…" Angela stammered.

"I think she's okay," he said.

"I'll take a look as soon as…" Dan paused. "Well, in a minute."

JeanBeth threw her arms around Lon, and Dan smacked him on the back. Candace couldn't get out one single audible word.

"Thank You, God," her soul shouted in silent jubilation. *"Thank You."*

Marco waited until Lon signaled that he'd gotten Tracy clear before he contacted Dev.

"In position?"

Dev clicked the radio to show that he was on the lower floor, working his way toward the boxing ring. They should be exiting and waiting patiently for the police to arrive, but Marco couldn't chance it. That was the second part of the plan, the part he hadn't divulged to Candace. If Rico escaped again, Candace and Tracy would never be safe. They would live constantly looking over their shoulders, their world darkened by the shadow of fear.

Rico must not be allowed to get away this time.

Gun in hand, Marco stepped into the gym, the smell of sweat and musty towels thick in the air. The light was dim, but sufficient for him to see that Rico was standing at the window, binoculars trained through the blinds, his back to the room.

Marco smiled and raised his weapon. "Watching for me? I'm flattered."

Rico whirled, hand going for his belt.

"Uh-uh," Marco said, his gun aimed at the gang leader's chest. "You know the drill. Keep your hands where I can see them."

Rico composed himself, jerking his chin. "Well, lookie here. Popeye is back."

"Face down, on the floor. Slowly."

"So you're a cop, too, Popeye? Navy SEAL, private eye and now officer of the law?"

"No, just gonna hold you here, tied up like a Thanksgiving turkey, until the cops arrive. It's good practice for you, since you're going to be locked up for the rest of your life."

Rico's eyes narrowed to dangerous slits. "I'm not going to jail."

"It's not your choice to make."

He laughed. "'Cuz you're the big bad hero come to take me in? I don't think so." His manner was cocky, sly. Marco scanned quickly but saw no signs of any other hostiles, and

Lon or Dev would have alerted him if there were. Sneakers squeaked against the tile. Rico heard it, too, his eyes darting toward the noise.

"What was that, you're probably wondering?" Marco said, a smile creeping across his face. "I'm pretty sure that's your hired gun getting a lesson on close-quarters combat from a friend of mine."

Rico glared.

"You were planning an ambush?" Marco shook his head. "You'd need more guys for that, a lot more, and we'd beat you anyway, just the three of us."

Dev strolled in, hauling Shoe Guy by the back of his shirt. The prisoner struggled, but Dev had his hands secured behind his back with a zip tie.

Marco laughed. "Hey, there. Nice to see you again. We gotta stop meeting like this."

The guy started in on a string of profanities until Dev nudged him in the back. "Such language," he said. "You need to work on that, my man."

Rico shot him a look of utter disgust.

"I didn't see him coming," Dev's prisoner muttered.

"'Course you didn't," Dev said with a grin. "I'm a SEAL, dude. That's like a superhero, only cooler."

"Bear's outside waiting," Marco could not resist adding. "He's been looking for you. He wants another shoelace to play with."

Dev's glance shifted to Rico. "Got this?"

"Right behind you. Secure your prisoner outside and Bear will watch him. Wave the cops in."

Dev exited with his captive. Marco edged nearer to Rico. "So where were we? That's right. You were getting down on the floor slow and easy."

Rico didn't move. "So you think it's over, huh?"

"Affirmative. You're done threatening Candace and Tracy and anybody else. Prison time."

"I got friends in prison," he spat.

"And you got people you crossed there, too."

Rage flickered in Rico's face. He threw down the binoculars and reached for his gun. Marco reacted, kicking out, catching Rico in the elbow, causing the weapon to drop to the floor. Marco launched it away with his foot and then he was crashing against him, pushing him against the wall, holding him secure with one hand while he checked for concealed weapons with the other.

"Game's over," he hissed into Rico's ear. "Good guys for the win."

Candace held Tracy so tightly she squirmed. "Mommy, you're squeezing me."

"I'm sorry." She didn't want to let her child out of her hold, but had a deep sense that it wouldn't be over until she witnessed Rico's arrest.

Dan drove the car to the front of the warehouse, where the police had set up a perimeter. Dev was keeping Bear in check at the end of a sturdy leash as the dog barked in displeasure at being kept again from his quarry.

"Where's Unco?" Tracy said, as Candace got out of the car.

"Stay with Grandma and Auntie Angela. I'll be right back."

"Candace…" Dan started.

"I need to see this," she said, and after a moment he nodded. She would be there when Marco took Rico from the warehouse. He'd already radioed in that he'd captured Rico and was bringing him out. Candace felt a burning desire to look into her tormentor's face when he was put into a police car. She moved forward a few paces until she was stopped by an officer.

"Stay back, please."

She looked past him to the gym. The door opened.

Marco pushed Rico past the threshold and he walked out, expression defiant, as if he didn't believe he was about to be arrested.

Believe it, Rico. You will never hurt me or mine again. Marco stood behind, his face obscured by his baseball hat. She hoped he felt the same heady sense of satisfaction that she did. Things would be different for them now, she felt, deep down inside. Joy, warmth, satisfaction, relief and love all mingled together in her soul.

An officer came forward to handcuff Rico.

She heard the snap of one cuff encircling his wrist and it sounded like music. After all the struggle and fear, they had won, beaten back the enemy and were safe. She would never take that feeling for granted again.

The cop suddenly jerked back as Rico grabbed the gun from his holster. He fired and the gunshot ripped through the night. Rico took off running in the direction of the car, head down, moving faster than she'd believed possible. Guns were drawn and aimed at Rico, but the cops didn't fire; they couldn't, without hitting the car or Candace.

She acted without thinking, grabbing the bat from the backseat. Her mother tried to hold her, but she broke free, whirled, and just as Rico brought the gun up to fire again, swung as hard as she could, her terror and fear all rolled into one massive stroke of the bat. She caught Rico in the knees. He tumbled over and over, coming to rest on his back, the gun skittering several yards away. He looked up at her, dazed and defeated, grunting in pain.

Tears stung her eyes and triumph, sweet and strong, swept her body from head to toe. "That's your last ring," Candace said, breathing hard. "Don't bother calling again."

The police surged forward and held Rico down while they properly cuffed him.

JeanBeth was out of the car, staring, stunned, her hands pressed to her mouth. Angela held Tracy, who was crying. Candace wanted to run to her, but something, some prickle of dread, made her turn. Behind the circle of cops, people were shouting, a sense of urgency in their voices. She moved forward slowly at first and then at a sprint, shoving past the cop who tried to stop her, all the jubilation she'd felt before morphing into a dark cloud of dread.

"What it is?" she panted. The cop standing nearest the gathered group didn't answer.

She saw Dev, face twisted under his bush of beard, Bear whining pitifully and hauling at the leash.

The cluster of officers parted.

Marco lay on the ground, limbs sprawled, eyes staring unseeing at the sky.

TWENTY-FIVE

Marco didn't feel pain in his chest where the bullet had plowed into him. His mind was oddly disconnected from his body. Blurry outlines of people flickered in and out, cops then paramedics. They removed his vest and began treating him, trying to stop the bleeding, he suspected, though he couldn't feel any of their efforts.

Odd, he thought, that he couldn't feel.

"No!"

He heard the cry and he knew it was Candace.

It's okay, he wanted to tell her. *Tracy is safe*. But his lips wouldn't move. Her face swam into his field of vision, stricken with grief, perfect brown eyes filled with tears that spilled down, splashing on his cheeks. How he wished he could experience the warmth of those tears.

"Marco!" she screamed.

He wanted to reach up and soothe her, to let his fingers linger in her unruly curls, but his arms wouldn't work.

A paramedic edged her aside. "Ma'am, step back now," he said.

Ask her, don't order her, Marco thought.

"Marco, don't you die, do you hear me?" she yelled at him. "Please—" Her voice broke. "Please don't leave me."

Yes, ma'am, he wanted to say, but now he was feeling something, a hard pain in his chest, as if someone had hammered a nail into his heart. The sensation deepened, expanding to strip away every other sensation except excruciating pain. The voices around him grew louder, more intense, and then there was nothing at all.

* * *

Two days after the shooting, Candace let Tracy see Marco for a few minutes. She had explained as best she could about the injuries Marco had sustained when Rico grabbed the cop's gun and shot him.

"Unco was hurt badly. He had an operation to fix his heart and he hasn't woken up yet."

"Is he gonna get better?" she asked with trembling lips. It hurt Candace to look at her.

The doctor's words came back to her. *Touch and go. Massive blood loss. Fifty-fifty.* "We're going to pray and God's going to decide."

"But what if He lets Unco die like Daddy did?"

Then Marco would die knowing that they cared about him, she and Tracy, but not knowing the full truth. Her own words to him came back in heart-wrenching detail. *I don't want you here, or in my life or Tracy's.* She swallowed hard and forced a calm mommy smile.

"It will be okay. I know Unco wants to see you, even if he can't say it." Her throat constricted and her palms shook as she kissed and hugged her daughter. She led her into the room where Marco lay, eyes closed, with an oxygen mask over his face, his chest bandaged and an IV affixed to his arm. Various monitors tracked his vital signs, beeping softly like a kind of monotonous music.

Tracy climbed up on a chair to kiss Marco on the forehead above the mask.

"Wake up, Unco," she said. "I want to talk to you."

But there was no flicker of consciousness from him, no twitch to indicate he knew they were there. Together they prayed for God to bring Marco back to them. Tracy sang him a song she'd learned from the music teacher at school about a monkey and a bunch of bananas.

When she sensed Tracy had had enough, Candace helped her down from the chair and urged her toward the door.

"Wait," Tracy said. She took from her pocket the little pink bunny Marco had made and pressed it into his hand, folding his thick fingers around the tiny wooden body. "I'll leave this to keep him company until he gets better."

Candace fought for composure. "I know he'd like that."

Angela took Tracy home to stay with their mother, and Candace settled into the chair next to Marco's bed. She straightened the sheets around his torso and traced a gentle finger over the healing scratches on his face.

Dev peeked his head in the door, looking ridiculously casual in baggy shorts, flip-flops and a T-shirt with Beach Bum emblazoned across the chest. He hardly seemed the same person who'd been bristling with battle gear only two days before.

"Hey, Gumdrop," he said. "Captain Ma'am said I'd find you here. Shipping out today since our bird is finally fixed."

She got up and hugged him tightly, fighting tears. "I never got to thank you for what you did getting my daughter back and helping Marco."

He looked at his feet. "Shouldn't have ended like that. Should have seen it going bad earlier."

"It's not your fault. More mine than anyone else's. He wouldn't have been involved in any of it if it wasn't for me."

"Aww, Chief wouldn't have wanted it any other way. Ever since I've known him, he's always talked about you and Tracy." Dev's expression was wistful. "I kinda wished I had something like that to come home to. It helps us do what we do, knowing that there's good stuff back home. You were that good stuff for Chief. Still are."

She bit her lip to keep from crying.

"Anyway, I just popped in to give my regards." He noticed the wooden rabbit poking out of Marco's hand. It sent him into a paroxysm of laughter. Candace watched, bemused, until his guffaws subsided and he wiped his eyes.

"What is so funny?"

"Old Boo-boo Bunny's got another rabbit in his hands."

She blinked at Dev. "What?"

His grin was mischief itself. He lowered his voice to a conspiratorial whisper. "That's Chief's nickname. When we first served together he was learning how to do woodcarving so he could make those rabbits for Tracy. He wasn't very good at it, at first, and he kept nicking his hands. Even needed stitches one time, so we called him Boo-boo Bunny. Oh man, the whole unit teased him mercilessly."

She could only gape. "You're kidding. Boo-boo Bunny?"

"Yep, and he threatened me and Lon with unimaginable bodily injury if we ever revealed this information to anyone."

Candace put her hand over her mouth to stifle a giggle. "I never would have guessed that, for sure."

Dev drew close to the bed. "Hear that, Chief?" he murmured in Marco's ear. "I just blabbed your nickname, so whatcha gonna do about it, huh?" His smile grew sad when there was no response. "Okay. You just sit there and take it. I'm shipping out anyway, but next time I'm in town, I'm gonna be disappointed if you don't make good on your threat, you hear?" He lightly squeezed Marco's shoulder and whispered, "Don't forget, Chief. Every time."

She knew he was reminding Marco of the SEAL creed. "When knocked down," she remembered Marco saying in the past, "I will get up…every time."

Dev kissed her cheek and left. Candace stood by Marco's bed, stroking his forearm.

"So now you've got to listen to me, don't you?" she said, her voice wobbling. "You're a captive audience, since you've decided not to awaken for a while. Well, I've got some things to tell you, Marco Quidel, and I'm not going to stop until you keep your word and get back up."

Swallowing down the tears, Candace began to talk. She

told him all the secret longings of her heart, which transcended guilt, the past and every other obstacle that had stood between her and Marco over the years. She talked and prayed for hours, as the nurses' shifts changed and the day turned into evening, thanking him for what he'd done for her, explaining how she'd learned about honor and sacrifice from him, from Rick, from her father.

When she ran out of words, she kissed his cheek, then laid her head against his chest and listened to the beating of his poor injured heart. "Are you ready to wake up now, Marco? For me and Tracy?"

There was no answer, and she was about to move so her tears wouldn't wet the sheets. Then she felt the pressure of Marco's big hand as he laid it gently on her shoulder.

"Marco," she breathed, throat tight. "You're alive." Joy enveloped her in a fierce grip.

"Mostly, anyway," he whispered.

She kissed his cheeks, his chin, his forehead, and finally his lips. Happiness coursed through her. God had spared his life. He kissed her back, so tenderly it was like a sweet breeze blowing through her soul.

Marco stroked her hair and pulled her face to his chest. His breath hitched in pain and her heart broke, thinking of how much anguish she'd caused Marco Quidel.

"Does it hurt very badly?"

He grimaced. "No worse than a hatchet to the sternum."

She cried some more, overwhelmed at seeing those copper eyes open again, his mouth smiling at her through the pain. "I love you," she heard herself say.

Wonder and confusion warred in his eyes. He put his hand behind her head and pressed her lips to his again. "I've always loved you, Candace," he said. "But I know that… I understand your heart belongs to Rick."

His name struck her like a blow. She felt dizzy, confused, unmoored. What was she doing? How could she have said she loved Marco? Guilt sliced through her joy. "I do love you," she whispered. "But I…"

"I understand. Really," he said. "You don't have to say it."

"I just can't let you replace Rick in our lives." Tears coursed down her face and onto the hospital sheets. "I'm so sorry."

"It's okay," he whispered. "It's okay."

But how could it be okay for her to love him so completely without betraying the memory of the man she'd promised to cherish until her dying day?

His arms were warm comfort around her back and she knew he forgave her for hurting him.

Relief, pain, longing, grief, guilt and love swirled inside until she felt dizzy.

She thanked God for the blessing Marco Quidel had been in her life, and offered heartfelt gratitude that his life had been restored.

Five days before Thanksgiving, Marco picked Bear up from the backyard at Donna's place, where the dog had been staying, and gingerly got in the truck to make his way back to the *Semper Fortis*. His chest burned with three-alarm pain, but he'd decided to leave the hospital in spite of the doctor's advice. He couldn't stand the way the Gallagher girls were tiptoeing around, talking softly and fussing with his blankets as if he wasn't even in the room. Sarah was back from her honeymoon, and since she was a surgical nurse, she'd taken to reading his reports and scanning his chart every day. Embarrassing.

More importantly, he was unsure of what was memory and what was a product of his surgery-addled mind. His brain replayed snatches of Candace caressing his face and speaking, her words tender, her voice thick with emotion. That was more than likely bits of daydreams that had lodged in his head, he figured. She'd said she loved him and he'd said the same, unless he'd imagined the whole thing. Her subsequent visits to his hospital room were awkward, her face flushed, her hands searching for things to do, their conversation strained. He remembered one phrase clearly. "I can't let you replace Rick in our lives." And he wouldn't want to. He'd allow his own happiness to end before he intruded on another man's family. In spite of his mending heart, he felt oddly dead inside.

Tracy was the only one who spoke in a normal fashion to him, poking a finger at his bandage and asking when he would be well enough to take her fishing. *Today, now, right now*, he wanted to tell her, but nothing had changed, not really. He was still leaving, only this time he could do it without any lingering worry. Rico was in jail and Champ had been arrested, also, for arranging their ambush at the chop shop. The Packs and Cliffs were busily clashing over top dog status, but that was a problem he'd happily leave for the police to sort out.

He parked at the marina and got out of the truck, an action that hurt way more than it should have, before he set off at a slow walk. Halfway to the dock, he sat on a bench to rest, grateful there were no people around to see him panting. Rico's shot had taken more out of him than Marco would ever admit to.

"Coming aboard?"

The voice startled him to a standing position. He thought he might be hallucinating at first, but it really was Candace Gallagher perched on the top railing of the dock in a pair of cutoff jeans and a short-sleeved T-shirt, his baseball cap trapping her curls. Bear galloped off to lick her shins in exchange for the nice ear rub she provided.

"What are you doing here?" he asked.

"The right question is 'How did you know I would be here at this moment, Candace Gallagher?' The answer is

I am a brilliant detective and I asked a friend who works the hospital to call me when you reached the end of your tolerance and broke out."

"Didn't break out. I left."

"Did you fill out discharge papers?"

He shrugged, a small gesture so she wouldn't see him wince. "Don't like paperwork."

"Naughty, Mr. Quidel. Very naughty."

He watched the wind play with her hair. Those curls had a life of their own in spite of all her efforts to mash them down. The wild coils suited her, so full of energy and fun. He shrugged, covering his pain as best he could.

She saw through his bravado, jumping down from the railing and moving to him, a frown of concern on her face. "Did they give you pain meds?"

"Yeah."

"But you didn't take any?"

"Don't need 'em."

She sighed. "You're going to be a difficult patient, aren't you?"

"Not a patient anymore," he said. "I'm going to cast off and head for Mexico."

"My mother sent orders that you are to stay with her until after Thanksgiving."

He chuckled. "I'm afraid this time I'm going to have to disobey the admiral."

"Risky."

"Yes, but I need to go. Thanks for coming to see me off." She was silent and he wasn't sure what else to say, so he walked slowly up the pier toward the *Semper Fortis*. "Oh, hang on." He fished the pink rabbit from his pocket. "Can you give this back to Tracy? Somehow it keeps winding up with me."

"Sure thing," she said. "Boo-boo Bunny."

Marco froze and his mouth dropped open. "Dev?"

She was laughing. “Yes, Dev.”

“I’m gonna clobber him when he’s stateside.”

“He’s counting on it.”

Marco could only smile, but he tried his best to hide it. Oh, how he was going to miss this woman who could make him grin like no one else in the world. Best not to think about it. He turned again to go.

“Since I know your deepest secret,” Candace said, “it’s time for you to know mine.” The laughter died away from her expression and he was struck by the sincerity that seemed to shine from her like a searchlight on the water. “I have to tell you something, and if you still want to leave after I say it, that’s okay.”

His stomach tensed up in that way that meant his life was about to change. He wasn’t sure what to think, or what to hope for.

“I’ve been doing a lot of praying and soul searching about what I said to you in the hospital, and I want you to know how much you mean to me,” she said.

He was confused. “I know you and Tracy care about me.”

“Yes. I mean, no, that’s not what I’m trying to say.”

He was going to rub a hand along his chin to give him something to do, but it hurt too much, so he lapsed into silence, the best way he knew how to deal with uncertainty.

She looked past the boat into the churning surf. “When I lost Rick, I thought my life was over, but it wasn’t, things continued on without him and I didn’t know what to do with the pain. I thought that in order to honor him, I had to hold on to his memory and wrap myself and Tracy in it, to keep away anything or anyone who might take our lives in a different direction.”

A bird skimmed the water beyond the boat.

Candace sighed. “But that’s not what Rick would have

wanted. It's not what God wants for me and for my daughter."

Something was dawning inside Marco that felt very much like hope, but how could that be? His past was such a wreck, his only solace came in knowing that Candace and Tracy had survived, unlike Gwen. "What...what do you think He does want?"

She turned her gorgeous eyes fully on him and he thought his heart would stop right then and there.

"He wants me to love a good man, a God-fearing man." She gulped. "You, Marco."

He stared, his breath growing short.

"God put you into my life and Tracy's, and my own stubbornness and fear has kept me from acknowledging the truth. The whole thing with Rico sort of blasted away any fears I had. He took me to the depths, where everything I leaned on was taken away and you were the one standing next to me, Marco. And you know what?"

"What?" he managed to rasp.

"I would not have wanted anyone else to be beside me but you. I finally understand that loving a good man does not take away anything I had with Rick." She put her hands around his neck. "I love you, Marco."

I love you, too, more than any other person in this world. He thought he'd said it aloud, but it must have been his soul shouting the words. He tried again. "I am not sure I'm worthy. I—I messed things up so badly the first time."

She cupped his cheek. "But God's given us both a second chance. Will you take it with me?"

He couldn't answer, so he found her mouth with his and kissed her, lighting a trail of joy that blasted away the past, the pain, the guilt. "I love you, Candace, and I love Tracy. I will always honor Rick's memory, but I want you to marry me and I want us to be a family, officially."

Her eyes shone as she looked up into his. "Are you sure

you can handle marrying into the Gallagher clan? We have a lot of determined women, you know."

"Yes, ma'am, but I'm a navy SEAL, so maybe I can hold my own at least from time to time."

"Good guys for the win," she said, eyes filled with tears as she looped her hands around his neck and encouraged him to kiss her again.

"I love you," he breathed against her neck, thanking God almighty for putting Candace Gallagher into his life.

"And I love you, too, Boo-boo Bunny."

Marco knew he would never hear the end of that atrocious nickname, never stop loving this determined, funny, faithful, earnest woman. He nuzzled her neck, relishing the brush of her curls against his cheek.

Boo-boo Bunny for the win.

* * * * *

If you enjoyed DANGEROUS TESTIMONY, look for the other books in the PACIFIC COAST PRIVATE EYES *series:*

DANGEROUS TIDINGS
SEASIDE SECRETS
ABDUCTED

Dear Reader,

I have had such a great time writing this series that takes place here on my beloved California coast. It was satisfying to explore the lives and loves of the four Gallagher sisters. Sisters are especially important to me, as I am one of four daughters. I am greatly blessed in that all my sisters live very close and I see them often. They are the people who share my joys and triumphs, and they are also the "3:00 a.m." people, as I like to call them. They are the folks you can call on in the middle of the night when disaster strikes, and they will be there to help in any way they can. Is there any greater blessing than that? I once heard someone say that friends come and go, but sisterhood lasts from cradle to grave.

I hope you have women like this in your life, dear reader, whether they are friends or sisters. It is a great joy to share this life journey with faithful women who will hold your hand, share your laughter and shoulder your pain.

Thank you again for journeying along with me through this series. As always, I enjoy hearing from my readers. You can find me on various social media spots—Facebook, Twitter, Instagram and Pinterest—but I also have a physical address on my website in case you would like to correspond by mail. Thank you for taking the time to read this book.

God bless you!

Dana Mentink